Return of the Mesomorph

James J. Caterino

Other published works by James J. Caterino include:
The Geek Girl and the Quarterback
Pop Songs or Poetry
Ready Set Action: The Best Short Fiction of James J. Caterino
Time Travel Stories
VHF: A Time Travel Story
The Promise
Pop Drawings
The Art of James J. Caterino
50 Films: Fifty Movies That Mattered to Me and Why
Pop Star
The Quarterback
Miami Noir 1987
Pop Culture Musings and Other Stuff

Chapter 1 - Super Villains

Carslon Getz sat in his throne-room styled office on the penthouse floor of Atlas Pharmaceuticals corporate headquarters on Brickel Avenue in Miami, rereading the classified report for the third time.

This is insane, he thought, like something out of a science fiction horror story or the plotline from the latest Marvel blockbuster.

A loner, low level research scientist named Dr. Anton Mason working in some college lab invents a rejuvenation formula in a syringe that works by rewriting the human genome codes backwards to a time when humans were more physically robust. When some opportunist mid-level suit decides to take over the project and throw the inventor under the bus, Mason goes rogue and continues his research by injecting himself with the formula.

After that is when the report starts to read like a comic book.

Witness accounts and even a police report that speaks of a rampaging man beast with superhuman strength who can leap over the top of patrol cars and travel through the trees like some kind of modern-day suburban Tarzan.

The term used in the report to describe Anton Mason after his transformation is "The Mesomorph". Even with that pseudo-scientific term thrown in there, the report really did read like pulp fiction.

Yes, it was insane. Batshit crazy to be sure.

But Getz was always one to see the big picture. He had bullied and blackmailed his way up to the executive suites. He had great predatory instincts and a keen eye for any opportunity that could benefit his bank account and his lust for power. His devious ambition knew no bounds.

He always found a way to get what he wanted, and right now, he wanted the CEO position at Atlas, and he would use that position to make the company and himself the most powerful player in the industry.

But there was an obstacle standing in the way by the name of Carrie Sune, a prodigy out of Stanford and an accomplished neurosurgeon. She was next in line to take the helm at Atlas after the Old Man finally retired. Those were the plans. The Old Man went on CNBC and said as much. But now, Getz had a way to change those plans. A way to get himself noticed. Noticed to the point where the board would have no choice but to give that power to him, and him alone.

In the report the formula was referred to as Meso48X and was part of something called Project De-evolution. And all of it was now the exclusive property of Atlas Pharma. As far as Getz was concerned, so was Dr. Anton Mason, or whatever it was that he was now.

But here was the rub. Whatever Dr. Anton Mason was, and by all accounts he was an eccentric loner, he was brilliant. Nobody else could crack his formula or make sense of his notes. Not even his top scientist Rachel Finn who he had taken great pains to lure into his plans. Dr. Finn said she needed a sample of original formula. And the only source left of the formula was now in Mason's bloodstream.

Getz could see it all coming together. Meso48X was his ticket to power and fame and everything he ever wanted. All he to do was find this man beast.

And he knew just the man for the job.

Getz hit the speaker on his phone.

"Julian. Send Krenshaw in here."

Chapter 2 – Keeper of the Wild

Anton shimmied out along the edge of the tree branch until he was in the perfect position to study the water in the canal below.

He allowed himself to be perfectly still and to be eternally patient. Two qualities that were essential for productive fishing. This was something he had learned from watching the pelicans, cranes, and various other exotic and beautiful birds of the Everglades.

He had learned so much from observing the wildlife around him. Ever since his transformation, he had a profound connection to the animals around him. It was so much more than just an instinctive connection. It was spiritual. Almost telepathic at times. He even bonded with a female panther he now called Luna because the first night they met it was under a bright full moon. In a stunning display of trust, she had walked up right next to him, and rubbed her head and shoulders against him, not unlike what a house cat would do.

Anton trusted animals far more than he ever did humans. He was able to see things and participate in amazing wonders because the animals did not see him as a dangerous human, but as a fellow creature of the wild.

That's what he was now. A creature of the wild. That is how he felt. That was how he thought, at least, most of the time.

But he also thought about his time as man. As a modern-day Homo sapien living in the twenty-first century Miami, Florida. As a human named Dr. Anthony Mason.

As Anthony Mason the human, he once had a life. He had parents and two sisters, and for a time when he was young, he even had friends. And toward the end of that life as a human, he had found the one holy grail of existence that every creature whether human or not has searched for.

Love.

He had found love in the form Amanda Zakori. And what had made their forced departure from each other all the more achingly painful was that she felt the same way about him.

If only he could find a way back to her. If only…

But a gaze down upon the still water below reflected his primitive image back at him, re-enforcing the reason why he could never go back.

His rejuvenation formula did what it was supposed to do, making him as robust, durable, and physically formidable as any human ancestor that had ever walked the Earth. But rewriting DNA, turning back the clock on human genome had a cascading and profound effects beyond anything Anton or any other evolutionary biologist could have ever predicted.

He now had the protruding jawline of a Homo Erectus, the dense bone structure of an over-sized Homo heidelbergensis, the hirsute, massively muscled torso of a gorilla, the mouth shape and the arm length of a chimpanzee or Australopithecus, and several times the suspected physical strength of a Neanderthal. And yet, he was none of those things, just as he was not human. He was, the Mesomorph, at least that was how he had coined it in his research.

But what was he? A resurrected hominid from the past? Or a new species? Or a one-of-a-kind freak accident of science? Perhaps, he was the famed missing link, that elusive common ancestor from which both the human and chimpanzee lineages split some 4.6 million years ago.

Whatever he was, Anton was hungry, and to his delight, he spotted a nice-sized largemouth bass rippling underneath the surface just below his reflection.

He dropped down from the tree branch, leading with the tip of the spear he held in his left hand. His reflexes were now lightning quick, and Anton had his prey on the tip of the spear before he broke the surface of the water. Once in the canal, he added two more fish to his collection before climbing up onto solid ground.

Downwind from him he spotted a black bear who had probably come to the canal for the same reason as Anton.

He looked at the size of the three bass skewered onto his spear and he realized they were much larger than he had anticipated. One would be more than enough for this evening's meal, along with the fruits and edible plants he had procured earlier today and had stored back inside the hollowed out giant oak tree trunk that he now called home.

He knocked two of the fish off the spear, then heaved them at the feet of the bear.

The creature was curious and surprised, but ultimately grateful. The bear dug into the first fish then let out roar of approval in his direction. Anton beat his left fist against his chest then raised it into the air as he answered the bear with a shout of "Anton" and then a roar that said, *I am Anton. I am a friend to the bear and all the creatures of the forest. You are Bass the Bear. You are my friend.*

Anton knew how insane it would sound if he ever said that aloud to anyone else. But deep down he knew, with absolute certainty, that the bear understood him in all the ways that mattered.

Anton often spoke aloud to the creatures of the forest and to himself. He did this not only to gain the trust and respect of the animals around him, but to physically exercise his voice.

The reverse evolution metamorphosis he had undergone had changed the shape and structure of his vocal cords and it was now difficult to enunciate words. This was the reason why, at least yet, even the most intelligent chimpanzees, gorillas, and orangutans, despite mastering sign language to a remarkable degree, had never spoken a human word. Some had theorized that it was because the shape and position of the vocal cords made it difficult, as it probably did almost all the hominids that proceeded Homo sapiens. Thus, Anton made an effort to speak every day in order to train his newly shaped chords and throat muscles.

He walked back up into the density of the forest where his oak tree home was. Inside the tree he kept a metal suitcase full of various supplies he had foraged from the side of I-75 near camping and rest stop locations. He found himself using those supplies less and less. A few of exceptions were a small portable metal grill and a knife. Although he already learned that his digestive system was now capable of digesting raw fish without getting sick, he still preferred it cooked. The grill had a lid and he placed it inside an overhang of stones he had constructed, so there was no danger of starting a fire nor any risk of someone spotting the flames from a distance or above.

As he filled himself on the sizable bass, apples, and wild dandelion, Anton listened to the soothing sounds of the wetland forest around him as darkness fell.

It was a symphony of birdsong, chirping creatures, moving water, swaying grass, and trees blowing about in a gentle humid breeze, as if it were all one giant biological orchestra. It all felt so warm, so peaceful, so right. His being, his very soul, was now infused with this place and the trees and creatures around him. It was a life-affirming connection of mind, body, and soul he had never felt in the human world. That is, with one exception.

Amanda.

Her beauty. Her warm, winning, funny personality. Her intoxicating, arousing smell that drove him mad with lust. And her passion as a lover as the two of them became joined as one. It was physical but all so much more. He craved her. He adored her. Just the way that she made him feel, like everything was suddenly wonderous and the world was full of hope and possibility. She was his first and only love. She haunted him.

His heart ached for her.

Feeling melancholy, Anton climbed up onto the thick, flat base branch of the strong oak and made a nest from leaves, branches, and vine, just as any great ape would.

Then he stared through the tree branches above him and up into the starry night sky until he fell asleep, dreaming about a world in which he and Amanda had a life together.

Anton awoke at sunrise and went about his day doing what he did every day; chewing a root which he had deduced must contain an alkaloid of caffein while patrolling the forest, foraging for food, and mapping out his surroundings until he could get to the point where he knew every last inch of the wilderness. This was his new home after all.

Today he explored northward, just below where I-75, a.k.a. Alligator Alley, cut across the southern width of the state. Amid his trek, he stuck paydirt in the form of a sprawling bush of perfectly ripe wild blueberries. He was picking off berries and gathering them into a shoulder satchel he had made with vine, when suddenly, he felt a jarring shift in the air around him.

The hair on his hirsute torso stood straight up. He felt an electric surge of involuntary adrenaline spike inside him.

Danger.

Someone was coming his way. Anton could sense them. He could hear them. Then, he could even smell them.

Humans.

They were invading his domain.

Anton had been a human. He knew all too well the evil and destruction that they brought with them.

He could here cackling, obscene, hideous laughter. Then shouting.

Then, he heard a scream. The scream of a terrified young girl.

Chapter 3 – A Paradise No More

Anton eyed up the tree line above him. Plenty of thick branches and dense foliage. Perfect.

He scampered up into the branches, leaping from tree to tree, straight toward the sound where the scream came from. He was there in seconds.

On the narrow trail below him he could see a young girl running, moving with a desperation, as if she were fearing for her very life.

The girl screamed out for help as she ran.

Coming up on her and closing the gap were three men dressed in camouflage. They were sizable men, and they were armed with rifles, long knives, and sidearms. Anton had been in the forest long enough now to know their ilk. Poachers. And in this case, would be rapists.

The intellectual part of Anton knew that revealing himself could only lead to bad things. But he was now a creature operating more on emotions, instincts, and primal drives. And now, he could only react in one way.

Must protect the girl.

He reached back and took out the spear strapped to his back with a harness he had made combining rope he had found with natural vine. Then, he watched as the girl's attackers drew closer and closer, until the precise moment arrived.

He dropped down from the tree branch, landing softly on his feet, placing his muscular, hirsute form directly between the running girl and her pursuers.

The first of the three men ran straight into Anton's right forearm while squealing "what the…" with a look of sheer horror on his face. The force of Anton's forearm into the man's chest knocked the wind out of adversary. He swatted the scumbag aside like a pesky fly, knocking him clear off the trail into a thick thorny bush.

The other two men were far enough behind the first to be able to stop. They just stared at Anton's fearsome presence. They stared in terror. They stared in disgust.

"Go!" Anton roared.

"Go!" he repeated.

He really did not want to kill them. He just wanted to keep them from hurting the girl. If only they would just leave. Then he could make sure the girl was okay and this whole thing could end before it escalated to a whole new level.

The man Anton had tossed aside was still dazed. Of the two men standing in the trail, one of them was white as a ghost, reeking of urine and feces. Anton could smell that the pale-faced coward had pissed and shat himself. But the other man, who wore a flannel shirt and was wearing a hunter's orange cap on his head, he was one of those assholes who just had to do what humans do. Try to destroy. Try to kill.

The hunter raised his rifle and pointed it at Anton.

In the same instant, Anton unleashed the spear with a whipping quick release from his left hand. The spear whistled through the air like a guided missile straight into the gun toting fiend's shoulder, knocking the rifle out of his hand.

It was a non-lethal blow. He really did not want to kill anyone. Part of it was moral. Part was practical. These men, as despicable as they were, probably had people who would miss them. People who would send the authorities looking for them. More humans with guns

He heard a rifle being hoisted behind him to the right. He hit the ground as a shot was fired.

It was the first man he had tossed aside.

With a lighting quick animal reaction and vicious speed, Anton moved along the ground on all fours. He was on top of his would-be murderer before there was a second shot.

He grabbed the rifle, and in a release of pent-up barbaric rage, he broke the gun in two. Then he picked up the befallen quarry at his feet, hoisted him in the air, and carried him back over to the main trail.

He dropped him next to the orange-capped hunter who was laying there moaning like a baby with the spear still sticking out of him. The man who had pissed and shat himself had fainted.

Real tough guys, Anton thought.

He pulled the spear out of Orange Cap. Then he bitch slapped the fainted man until he was awake. All three of the invading attackers were now on the ground at his feet, quivering like the cowards they were.

Anton stood above them, and he roared.

It was a deep, primal, rage-filled barbaric cry of dominance that declared in no uncertain terms that it was he, Anton the Mesomorph, who ruled the wetland forests of South Florida, and not these weak, pitiful, hate-filled destroyers of life like these three pathetic humans.

"Go!" Anton screamed at them, holding his spear locked and loaded on his left shoulder in case any of them reached for a knife or handgun.

"Leave!" he yelled. "And don't ever come back. Ever!"

All three of the cowering humans scampered fearfully to their feet and scurried down the trail back toward I-75 as fast as their beaten, bruised, and in one case impaled, bodies could manage.

Anton roared one more time, because he had to.

His primal rage was a bottomless pit. He wanted to kill these evil men so bad, it ached, and he began to wonder if he had made a mistake by trying to do the right thing and letting them live.

Then, when the roar ended, he turned around, began to move back into the woods, and there she was standing right before him.

It was the girl.

Chapter 4 – Sarah

Anton tried to turn away and just vanish into the woods, but the girl called out to him.

"Please don't go," she said.

"It's okay," she said. "Please…stay."

Anton stopped.

Somehow, he felt the need to stay. Out here, this far away from whatever campsite she was at, the girl still might not be safe. The three men that he had dealt with were certainly not the only evil humans predators who lurked about at the edges of these woods.

He turned back toward the girl.

Despite the dirt, scrapes, and bruises from her ordeal, she was very pretty with dark hair that came to her shoulders. She was young, but perhaps a bit older than he had thought. Anton guessed about sixteen.

"Thank you," she said. "For what you did for me. If you hadn't helped…I don't even what to think about what would have happened…so thank you. So much."

He nodded at her.

"My name is Sarah," she said pointing at herself.

"And you are?" she asked, motioning over to him.

Anton stayed silent. He could not decide if speaking to her was such a good idea. He had determined that the less interaction he had with humans the better. But this time with this girl, it felt different,

"I know you can speak. I heard you back there. Well, I think half the state did," she said. "But how is that possible? I mean, I know that chimps and gorillas and orangutans can learn to sign, but talking? Did someone at a research center teach you? Are you from a sanctuary? Like the one up by Fort Pierce? Or from the Miami Zoo?"

She must have thought he was some sort of escaped chimpanzee or gorilla. Well of course she did, he thought. She would not have any other reference. It's not like she could have ever seen a Homo heidelbergensis or Home erectus or a Neanderthal or a, whatever he was.

"Are you lost?" Sarah asked. "Can I help you find your way back home?"

"Anton," he said, deciding to engage. "My name is Anton."

She looked at him with wide-eyed wonderment and complete astonishment.

Anton waved about at the forest around him.

This…this is home," he said. "Anton's home."

"Wow," she said, continuing to look at him as if she were totally captivated by his presence.

"You should go," he said.

"Oh yes…my God, Karl. He will be worried sick," she said. "That's my friend I came out here with. He wanted to do some fishing and I really don't have the patience for it, so I decided to go for a short hike and well, you saw what happened. Creeps."

"I will shadow you from the trees," Anton said. "Make sure you get back to Karl safely."

"Really? Wow…and thanks again…Anton," she said.

She started to walk but turned back toward him again.

"Please, Anton…let me do something for you to pay you back for saving me," she said. "There has to be something. Anything?"

Anton thought about it. And the thought he had was one based purely on emotion. An idea that involved risk. A lot of risk. But still, he had to try. This might be the only chance he ever had.

"There is one thing," Anton said. "One thing you can do for me."

"Just name it," Sarah said.

Anton took a deep breath, knowing he was about to cross a line he swore he never would.

"I need you to get a message to someone," Anton said. "Someone, special."

Chapter 5 – Amanda

Amanda Zakori went about her day as she always did, with extreme caution.

Ever since she had Anton's transformation, they had been watching her. And sometimes, they did more than watch, as was the case last week when a team of goons was sent to pressure her from Atlas Pharma. She refused to cower to them. She would not be intimidated.

"Tell Getz to go fuck himself," she told the henchman.

She knew Getz from her time working in the research lab. He was a jerk back then and an even more of an asshole now that the conniving prick had managed to acquire power by sliming his way up the corporate ladder.

Carlson Getz was everything that was wrong with the human species. He was greedy and destructive and cruel. But tragically, he did have power now and that made him dangerous. Dangerous to her. And most of all, dangerous to Anton.

Anton had been right to force himself to cut all ties to her and to keep her in the dark about his whereabouts. It was the only way to assure that they did not use her to get to him. It was the only way to keep them both safe. Because if they found him, they would put him in a cage and worse. So yes, it was the right choice. The smart choice. It was also the wrong choice.

It was wrong but it was so achingly painful. Not just having to say goodbye to him, but also the not knowing.

It been over a year now and she had no idea where he was. And she had no idea if he was even still alive. The not knowing, that was the worst part. It made every day a mental and emotional mountain of pain for her to endure. She missed him. She missed him so bad there were times when she could not catch her breath.

She tried to rebuild her life. She tried to go on. She really did. She left research and went back into teaching, taking a position at South Dade Community College. But the emotional hangover and the melancholy of the hole in her heart was there each and every day.

One day, Amanda was on her way to her office to read some student papers in between classes, when she sensed something was off.

Someone was following her.

She looked up into a window to catch a reflection of who was behind her. She expected to see an enforcer from Atlas or one of the other big pharma corps, but instead caught sight of a student. A young girl who seemed to be tracking her.

Amanda casually and nonchalantly made her way up to her office, hoping it was just what it seemed. A student seeking her out to speak to her about a classroom issue. But still, she did not recognize the girl as a student in one of her classes. Something was up.

There was only one way to find out.

She allowed the girl to catch up to her before making a hard left turn into her office. A moment later, there was a soft knock on the still open door.

"Come on in," Amanda called out, taking a seat behind her desk.

A pretty girl with dark hair rounded the corner and locked eyes with her. She had a knapsack slung over her right shoulder and carried an old school paper notebook in her left hand. She did seem to be a student. She looked young, even for a freshman. And there was an urgent seriousness in her eyes.

"Professor Zakori?" she asked.

"Yes," Amanda said. "How can I help you?"

"I just wanted to ask you about some things from yesterday's class," the girl said. Then she went over to close the door before sitting down across from Amanda.

There it was again. The desperate look on her face. The girl was nervous. Maybe even scared.

"Except I don't recognize you from any of my classes," Amanda said. "And I have a photographic memory for faces."

"So really," Amanda said. "Who are you and why are you here?"

The girl took a moment and looked around the room. She even inspected the land line phone on her desk.

"My name is Sarah," she said. "And…"

Sarah looked around, scoping out the room with a paranoid gaze.

"Is it safe to talk in here?" Sarah asked.

Amanda felt her heart race.

Who was this girl?

Amanda had all tracking functions and apps removed from her phone. She had changed her number three times over the last year. As far as she knew both the office and her phone were clean. As an extra precaution she took out her phone and powered it off in front of the girl.

"Now you?" Amanda said.

"I didn't even bring mine," the girl said. "I was warned."

"Warned? By whom?" Amanda asked.

"By Anton," the girl said.

Just hearing her speak his name had an instant and profound effect on her.

A cascade of emotions smothered Amanda. Shock, surprise, elation, hope, and heartbreak, all swirling together. Her heart raced even more. She could hardly breathe.

"Is he…" she could barely speak.

"Yes, he's okay," Sarah said. "That's why he sent me to find you. To deliver a message. That's he's alive and okay."

Amanda felt herself let a deep sighing breath of relief as her eyes filled with tears.

"And he wanted me to tell you that he thinks of you every day, and he dreams of you every night," Sarah said. "And that he loves you, Amanda. He loves you so much."

Sarah got up from her chair, came over to Amanda, and hugged her.

"Was that part of his message?" Amanda asked.

"No, that was from me," Sarah said. "You looked like you could use a hug."

"Yes," Amanda smiled and chuckled. "Yes, I did need that. Thank you."

"You're welcome, Amanda," Sarah said.

A nice moment passed between them. She seems like a wonderful kid, Amanda thought. Of all the humans Anton could have come across, she was glad it was someone like her. But he would not have looked for contact with any people, nice or otherwise. Avoiding all humans, that was the point of his exile.

"Sarah, how did you meet him?" Amanda asked.

"He saved me," Sarah said. "My friend and I were fishing at a rec area off I-75 near the Cypress Creek reserve. I went for a hike down a trail to the south and these three creeps with guns started following me and saying all the sort of things that creeps say. Before I could even realize what was happening, they were on me, trying to get me on the ground."

"Oh my God…honey I'm so sorry," Amanda said.

"I fought them. Bit one. Kicked one of them in the balls hard," she said. "Got free, and then ran. But they would not stop. They kept coming after me. Getting closer and closer. I kept screaming for help. And that's when he came."

"Anton?" Amanda asked.

Sarah nodded. There was a wide-eyed look of wonder on her face.

"Swooping down from the treetops above, like some sort of superhero," Sarah said. "He was magnificent."

"He saved me Amanda; he really did. And I could tell he purposely tried not to kill those dirtbag rapists. Even though they deserved it. But he made his point. You should have seen those losers running away, squealing like little babies."

Amanda felt herself smile. Even after the transformation, Anton was still a good guy. He was still…Anton.

"We talked after and he was…well, just the fact that he could talk, I'm still wrapping my brain around that," Sarah said. "How did he get so smart? I mean, he is like Caesar from *Planet of the Apes* smart. How did that happen?"

She thinks he is a chimpanzee or gorilla, Amanda thought. That made sense. His transformation must be complete now and settled somewhere in the five million years ago range. An ancient hominid from the past.

"It's…it's a long story Sarah," Amanda said. "And the less you know, the easier it will be to keep you safe."

"And right now," Amanda added. "That is what we need to work on. Starting with a cover story as to why you are here."

"Piece of cake," Sarah said. "I want to come here and major in biology with a special emphasis on anthropology. And I needed to get special permission to sit in on one of your classes. As well as advice about what pre-college courses to take for my senior year."

Amanda smiled and nodded.

Kind and smart.

Yes, she was happy that of all the humans he could have met up with, it was this girl, Sarah. She was so glad Anton had saved her.

Now, Amanda needed to find a way to keep her safe, no matter what.

Chapter 6 – Getz and Krenshaw

Krenshaw checked the balance in his account to make sure all the funds were there, and indeed they were, the entire two million.

The funds appeared to have come from some anonymous source in the Cayman Islands. Probably an Atlas Pharma dirtbag account that Getz set up to pay the kind of people who should best be left off the official payroll. People like Krenshaw.

"You'll get he rest when he is captured," Getz said.

Why hunting down Anton Mason was worth this much money to Getz, he had no idea. Well, he did know, it just seemed too preposterous for a hard ass like Krenshaw to believe.

A scientist who was now an ape of some sorts with the secret to immortality in his bloodstream? Really?

He was used to operating in the shadowy world of disinformation and dictators. If you wanted an election fixed, Krenshaw was your guy. He would do it, not by messing with ballots or voting machines, but by packaging a set of lies and repeating them over and over until enough people in the population was radicalized enough to believe them, or anything else that Krenshaw and his team of operatives around the world wanted them to believe.

Besides the hackers and the propagandists, Krenshaw also had connections to paramilitary groups all over, especially here in South Florida. Between his computer skills and the physical tracking abilities of those groups, he could find anyone on the planet, including this beast man Anton Mason.

He had a name. A probable, although vast target area, somewhere in the wilderness between the two coasts of Florida. All he needed now was a solid lead.

Getz insisted that a woman whom Mason was involved with, Amanda Zakori was the key. But he had surveillance on her for months, visual, audio, and personal, and there had been absolutely no contact between her and Mason. He had even personally interrogated her on several occasions and came up empty. Not because she was impossible to crack. But because she really did have no idea where he was. Krenshaw could spot a liar in an instant and Amanda Zakori had not lied to him during the interrogations.

The Everglades and all the various state and national parks to the north was just too much territory to blindly send out search parties. So, the hunt for Anton Mason the beast man was at a dead end.

The trail was cold. Until it wasn't.

A message came into Krenshaw over one of the encrypted secure apps on his phone. It was a link to a posting from a thread on Reddit.

It was a forum for gun fetishists and hunters and some loudmouth was boasting about his encounter with a "gigantic swamp monster."

"It must have been the Skunk Ape," another user replied.

"Yes, the Florida Bigfoot!" another said.

"Well, whatever it was, I taught it a lesson," the original poster said. "It's probably dead."

Krenshaw messaged back his contact, instructing her to put a tracer on the poster. He would have this yahoo in his custody within hours.

"Okay Mister Bigfoot hunter. Let's find out just how full of shit you are."

Getz fist pumped the air as he held the phone to his ear.

He was ecstatic.

This was the news he had been waiting for. He was now but one step away from getting everything he wanted. The power. The recognition. And most of all, the means to strike back at anyone who, at least in his narcissistic mind, had ever slighted him in any way.

Several hours later, Krenshaw called him back with an update.

"I'm through interrogating the hunter," Krenshaw said. "What a pussy. He sang like a canary. The real story is this asshole is a pedophile. He and his two inbred buddies were trying to rape some young girl. Your beast man interceded, disarmed all three of them and kicked their sorry asses all the way back to Miami."

"Yes, the girl," Getz said. "Now it makes sense. He would have strong, primal protective instincts. That is why Mason risked exposing himself."

"If this girl is his kryptonite, we should find her and use her as bait," Krenshaw said. "Make him come to us."

"I don't know. She might be a pain in the ass to find. The board meets here next week so I don't have time to waste," Getz said. "We can use Amanda Zakori. He'll come for her too. Believe me. And as an added bonus, I get to see the look on her face when we put that freak in shackles."

"That woman is unpredictable. So are relationships. Too many unknowns," Krenshaw said.

"What do you suggest?" Getz asked.

"We know he will protect this young girl. We use her," Krenshaw said.

"But, can you find her?" Getz asked.

"The hunter was very specific about the location of the incident and in the description of the girl. There is a recreation area near that spot, right off Alligator Alley. Twenty-four-hour security cameras all over the parking lot," Krenshaw said. "I'll find her."

Yes, Krenshaw was right, Getz thought. Amanda Zakori was a pain in the ass and would fight back and who knows if she and Mason worked out something ahead of the time to throw them off. She might even be willing to sacrifice herself to protect him.

Ahh, but this girl. Mason had already proven he would not hesitate to come out of hiding to protect her.

"Okay, do it," Getz said.

"I'll get my team ready," Krenshaw said.

Yes indeed, Getz thought. He was one step away.

One step away from being in control of the most powerful pharmaceutical company on the planet.

23

Chapter 7 – Abduction

The more Amanda thought about it, the more she realized she had to do something. Something to protect Sarah.

As careful as Sarah had been when seeking her out, not bringing her phone was no guarantee that somehow Getz and his goons had not found out about her. For all Amanda knew, they had someone right there on campus, in her building, or even right there in the Biology Department watching her every move, including who came in and out of her office.

Then there was the matter of the three dirt bag hunter rapists who had attacked Sarah. While Amanda was relieved that Anton had retained his core goodness after physically evolving backward millions of years into the past, she feared that allowing the attackers to live may have been a mistake.

While researching Krenshaw, the slimy silk-suit wearing thug who led the interrogation team who kept harassing her, she found out that Getz's chief enforcer had been on both the FBI's and the CIA's radar for years for orchestrating coups in Eastern Europe on behalf of Putin and for interference into U.S. elections. If these asshole hunters went around blabbing about their encounter with Anton, and surely they did, there was a good chance Krenshaw may have picked up on it.

There were just too many loose ends when it came to Sarah's safety. Staying away was not the answer.

Amanda had to do something. Maybe find a way to allow to her sit in on one of her classes. Maybe act as a tutor for her. Someway to keep a close eye on her and protect her from Getz.

She had memorized Sarah's contact info and made the girl do the same with hers. In case Amanda was just being paranoid, a call or a text was an unnecessary risk. She needed to go see Sarah in person.

It was early afternoon on a weekday, so she would still be in school. Amanda jumped into her car and headed out to the Miami suburb of Kendall.

Getz sat in the back seat of the black SUV limousine monitoring the screen on the tablet in his hand. He had ordered his driver to pull right up to the front of the high school.

Maybe it was a risk for him to be here right smack in the center of a clandestine operation that was essentially a kidnapping. But this was too important for him not to be here in person. He was so close now to getting everything he wanted. Nothing could be left to chance. He even had a very special person here with him to lure the girl out of class and into his waiting car. His chief scientist at Atlas, Rachel Finn. As with all of his underlings, he owned her.

Through carefully planned casual conversations, Getz came to learn the brilliant researcher was almost as ambitious as he was, and she was desperate to make a name for herself. Cracking the Mesomorph code and replicating the formula was catnip to the young, driven, ruthless biologist. And her friendly appearance along with some gibberish about some made up science fair invitation, was a nice angle that Finn should be able to sell well enough to put the young girl at ease. Or at least lure out of the classroom.

It was now only a matter of time.

Amanda spotted the security cameras mounted up on the light pools and tried to pick a spot in the rear parking lot that appeared to be in a dead zone, outside the video coverage.

She waited until she spotted a gym class heading back inside through the rear entrance, and as nonchalantly as possible, blended in with them and walked right inside the school. After all, Amanda was a college professor who looked the part, and if anyone stopped her, she was here to recruit potential candidates for the "pre-college credits program".

And when she was stopped and questioned by a security guard, she sold the cover story with ease and was directed to the principal's office, where she needed to go anyway since she had no idea what class Sarah would have been right now.

Her legitimate looks and the story sold so well; the principal saw her right away.

"Hi, I'm Dr. Rosen," the woman behind the desk said, rising to shake her hand. "What can I do for you Dr. Zakori?"

"Actually, I'm hoping to be able to something for you by helping out a few of your students," Amanda said. "By opening up some of my classes to high school students who have demonstrated a true passion for biology, and specifically my areas of expertise, anthropology and evolution."

"Oh? And why us?" Dr. Rosen asked.

"Because I actually got the idea from one of your students who came to me with a request to sit on one my classes," Amanda said. "A very bright, energetic girl who really has a love of anthropology. Her name is Sarah. Sarah Hoffer."

The principal's face lit up. Amanda could tell that Dr. Rosen must be a fan of Sarah's. Thank God.

"If it is possible for me to talk with her, that would be a very big help," Amanda said.

"Of course, Professor Zakori," Dr. Rosen said, tapping the keyboard on her desk while glancing at the screen.

"She's in Jim Stokes' history class right now," Dr. Rosen said. "I'm sure Mr. Stokes will not mind if we borrow Sarah for a few minutes."

Dr. Rosen got up from behind the desk and led Amanda out of the office.

"The classroom is right down the hall on this floor," Dr. Rosen said. "Come, I'll walk you there."

Amanda did not say much on the walk to the classroom. She knew herself well enough to know that she was a lousy liar, and the less she spoke the better. At this point Dr. Rosen was curious, but not quite suspicious. But as they turned a corner, it was Amanda who felt suspicious.

There were two people down at the end of the hall, walking away from them. A black woman crisply dressed in a business suit holding a briefcase. And by her side, a female student.

It was Sarah.

"Sarah!" Amanda called out.

Both Sarah and the woman escorting her turned. Amanda recognized the woman. It was Rachel Finn, the Atlas scientist who Getz assigned to recreate Anton's Mesomorph formula.

"Amanda?" Sarah answered back.

Rachel Finn must be a better liar that her. Sarah looked confused. She had no idea what kind of danger she was in.

Rachel Finn pulled Sarah in close to her. They both disappeared around the corner.

"Call security," Amanda said to Dr. Rosen. "Do not let them off school grounds."

Dr. Rosen said something about not understanding and asking what was going on. Amanda ignored her and moved down the long hallway as fast as she could, launching herself into a full sprint by time she reached the corner.

She planted her left foot to stop and make the sharp right turn to follow Finn and Sarah out into the lobby. As she made the turn, she was blindsided by a body blow.

Amanda found herself flat on her back, staring up at the ceiling, the wind knocked out of her.

Before she could recover a large man dressed in a suit hovered over, placing a wet, chemical smelling rag over her face.

Amanda felt herself fall into unconsciousness as everything went black.

Chapter 8 – Invasion

Anton spent half of his day doing what all wild hominids did, even humans up until about ten thousand years ago; foraging for food. The other half of his day was dedicated to the same thing he had been intently focused on ever since those scumbag rapist hunters had invaded his domain, creating weapons and devising traps.

It was only a matter of time now.

Only a matter of time before more evil humans invaded, and next time they would specifically be looking for him.

Murderous hunters, slimeball wannabe P.T. Barnum hucksters, big Pharma, or some insidious government research program. Any or all of them might invade this paradise any day now, and they all would have one goal in mind. To put Anton in a cage.

He was never going to let that happen. And when the humans came this time, he would not be as merciful as he was with Sarah's attackers.

Sarah.

Anton thought about the young girl How brave she was. He wondered of she was able to get his message to Amanda. Even a delayed, long-distance communication delivered by a third-party stranger was something. Anton needed to be able to reach out to Amanda any way he could safely. He wondered if that message he gave to Sarah might be the only chance he ever had.

He finished sharpening the spear in his hand, the held it up over his shoulder into the throwing position to get a feel for the aerodynamic balance.

The spear felt strong, straight, and light in his hand. Like he could kill a mosquito with it from fifty yards away. It was perfect. And it was one of several dozen of a variety of spears he now had ready. Spears for distance. Spears for medium range. And heavier spears for up close hand to hand combat.

Then there were the traps he had set. Snares, sinkholes, and even some strategically placed beehives. Anton made sure he had thoroughly urinated around all the traps to keep any innocent animals from wandering into the danger. At this point, Anton had established his reputation of dominance in the forest and when he left his smell on something it sent a message to stay away.

Now, it was time for the humans to be sent a similar message. This was his domain. His home. And he would protect it.

No matter what.

Amanda wheezed, sending her into a coughing fit that slapped her wide awake.

She opened her eyes to blurry vision that gradually came into focus. Her temples throbbed. Whatever they doused that rag in that, whether chloroform or something else, it had the side effects of a nasty hangover but worse.

She could feel herself moving and hear the humming drive of an engine and the sounds of tires on the road. She must have been in the back of truck or van. It was dark all around her, practically pitch black except for light bleeding in from the edges of two blacked out windows at the rear of the vehicle.

Sarah.

She had failed to protect the girl.

Amanda felt a horrible sense of panic and dread wash over her. Getz must have found a way to track her down, probably from the hunters just as she had feared. If only she had been able to get there sooner.

Now Getz had the perfect bait to capture Anton.

Why am I even still alive?

Probably as a backup. An extra insurance policy.

How was she going to get out of this? How was she going to be able save Sarah and protect Anton from a cage-ridden life of torture?

It felt hopeless, but she as long as she was alive, she had to try and find a way. She just had to.

Getz was sitting in the back seat of a black sedan with Krenshaw as they followed the van with Amanda Zakori and the car with Rachel Finn and the girl. Behind the sedan Getz and Krenshaw were in there was another van containing Krenshaw's assault team and all the weapons they would need to take down the beast man Mason.

"Alive," Getz reminded Krenshaw. "I need him that way, at least until Dr. Finn has what she needs to recreate the Mesomorph formula.

The van with Zakori was leading their mini caravan as they turned right onto the ramp that led down into the recreation area parking lot. The one from where Krenshaw had used security camera footage from to get an I.D. on the girl via the license plate of the car that she got in and out of that day/

They had the bait. They had the location. But still, Getz was nervous. He was not so convinced about Krenshaw's plan.

"You sure about this?" he asked.

"Relax Getz," Krenshaw said. "You really are a tightly wound mother fucker."

"Yeah? And one that pays well. Don't forget that," Getz said.

"Oh, I won't," Krenshaw said. "The second that savage is in your custody, I expect to check my phone and see that my bank account is full and fat from the balance of what you owe me."

"Don't worry about my end," Getz said.

"But I have to tell you Krenshaw," Getz added. "You are one cold bastard, sending your men in there after him. You're playing right into his hands. He'll kill them all."

"No he won't. At least not on purpose," Krenshaw said.

"Why would he spare anyone who came in there after him pointing a gun?" Getz asked.

"Because he's not a killer," Krenshaw said. "If he was, those three inbred asswipes would be decomposing somewhere deep in the Glades, or sitting half-digested inside the belly of a gator."

"Mason is not like you or me. He cares," Krenshaw said. "That is his weakness. That is how we found him. And that is how I will capture him. Alive, as you wish."

Getz nodded in agreement.

"But why not do it my way? Simple stupid style. Just take the girl up to the edge of the woods and make her scream for her life," Getz said. "He'll come."

"Yes, he'll come. But he'll be at full strength," Krenshaw. "He may have the strength of five humans or whatever, but he is flesh and blood. Having to deal with my men will get him good and tired. When he comes to us, I want him exhausted."

"Interesting strategy," Getz said. "You learn that working for Putin?"

"No. From comic books," Krenshaw said. "That's how Bane defeated Batman."

The car came to a stop and the divider between the front and back seat came down.

"We're here boss," the driver said.

"Okay Krenshaw," Getz said. "You're up. Don't let me down."

At first, he could hear their sounds. Humans were so loud. Every step was a crushing thud. Every breath an audible gasp.

Then, as they closed in on him, he could smell them.

As he feared, the humans were here.

Anton secured the two satchels of spears tied to his torso, pulled himself up into the oak, and climbed up into a secure, camouflaged position with a perfect view of the perimeter.

He could see the invading humans. These were not shit-kickers looking for a thrill kill. This was a paramilitary operation. Trained militia. Lots of men. Lots of guns. He was going to have to move fast and be very precise to have any chance.

One of the men stepped into a snare and was jerked skyward until he hung upside down from a tree branch, dropping his rifle and losing his weapons belt in the process. One down, and dozens to go.

The battle was on.

Anton gazed down from his hidden perch on the tree branch, waiting with a steely discipline until a group of the militia, with their fingers on the trigger and their rifles pointed ahead, walked into his throwing range. He waited as they came closer and closer, making certain the handmade missiles he launched could be delivered with pinpoint accuracy.

Then the moment arrived.

He unleashed a series of lightning quick tosses.

Spear after spear sizzled down through the air striking with a thudding pop into clavicles, biceps, forearms, and thighs. He hit every one of them twice. Once to force them to drop their gun. And once to take out their ability to chase after him.

The throws were intended to be non-lethal but cause maximum pain. Each of the men he struck squealed and grabbed for their wounded area causing them to drop their rifles.

Anton dropped down from the tree, hit the trail floor, and in a furious blur of motion, scooped up the loose automatic weapons, and jumped into the dense foliage of the forest as sprays of sub-machine gun fire chased after him.

He dumped the guns into the deep murky water of a canal and scampered back up into the trees with a blinding quickness and an insane agility that would make any primate on the planet envious. Then, using the treetops to launch himself through the forest to stay ahead of the sporadic gunfire, Anton worked his way to the next stash of spears.

The militia men kept firing blindly and tried to track him. Perfect. That was wanted.

There were cursing shouts and more screams as the men ran into more booby traps until Anton looked down and could see the number of his attackers had dwindled down to only a half dozen.

Then, he unleashed a new wave of spears, rocketing the hand made projectiles down at his enemies with a frightening velocity. Another run of scooping up guns, a dump into a small lake, then a return to the trees.

No more gunfire. No more men moving down the trail. Only the screams of pain from his fallen enemies.

The threat had been neutralized. But, still, Anton felt more anxious than ever. That had been too easy. Something else was happening. He was sure of it.

The sound of megaphone blasting through the air, shouting out his name, confirmed his fears.

"Mason!" the voice shouted.

It was a male voice. One he recognized from his previous life. Someone from a pharmaceutical company whom had showed an interest in his work.

"Mason, you have something I need," the megaphone man said. "And I have something that I think you need. Two females I know you care about."

Sarah! Amanda!

Anton felt a raging, savage anger boil up inside him.

"I know you can move fast, so I will only give you thirty seconds," the megaphone man said. "Thirty seconds until I start taking a knife to these pretty ladies. They won't be so pretty when I get done with them."

Anton exploded into action, moving toward the direction of the megaphone sound with such lighting speed and sheer dynamic force, he felt like he could run through a concrete wall. And if he had to, he would. He would destroy anyone or anything that dared to threaten Amanda or Sarah.

Sprinting up the trail using combination all fours and bipedal power, he rocketed into the clearing. He could see the man with megaphone. Next to him were Amanda and Sarah. They looked terrified. There was a militia man holding rifles to their heads.

Acting on pure instinct and rage, Anton reached back for a spear from the satchel still strapped to torse and whipped the spear straight into the militia man's chest as hard as he could. Showing mercy and sparing lives was no longer on his mind.

"Anton! Watch out!" both Amana and Sarah cried out in unison.

Several dozen men came out from the left and the right, each of them equipped with a taser gun they fired at him. Painful jolts of electric shock struck his flesh, shattering his nervous system, again and again. The men and the tasers kept coming at him, but Anton fought back against the thudding pain with primal fury and adrenaline.

He turned, lowered his shoulder, and bull-dozed into the group of men to his left, beating them with his fists, snapping their necks with the brute force of his strength. Then he took their fallen bodies and used them as a projectile weapon, heaving them into the group of men to his right as if they were bowling pins.

He kept fighting, crushing anyone he could get his bare hands on. He was determined to eliminate any threat to Amanda and Sarah. If he had to rip every one of them to pieces, he would. Such was his savage rage.

But then another wave of men attacked from both sides. Then another.

This time they were armed with electric cattle prods. Anton could feel himself getting jabbing shocks from every angle, straight into his flesh, over and over again. No matter how many men he crushed with his bare hands as he fought back, more kept coming.

He was surrounded.

More men. More cattle prods.

More pain than he could have ever imagined.

He could hear Amanda crying out.

He could hear Sarah sobbing.

He fought to get through the men. To somehow find a way to Amanda and Sarah.

But the sheer number of men. The insane amount of pain.

It was all too much.

Anton collapsed.

A huge steel net fell over him.

He felt a giant syringe get jammed into his shoulder.

Then, everything went dark.

Chapter 9 – The Cage

Anton awoke to find himself face down, staring into a concrete floor.

As he struggled to push himself up onto all floors, every limb, his entire torso, and most of all his head, felt like hell. He noticed a bandage and a special kind of soreness in between his bicep and forearm right on the vein they would have used to extract his blood.

He fought through the pain throbbing in the back of his neck, raised his head, and stared out through a wall of thick steel bars. On the other side of the bars there was a face he recognized from earlier, the leader of the militia, the one who was holding a gun pointed at Amanda and Sarah.

"If you harmed a single hair on either one of their heads…" Anton growled.

"Easy big guy. They were just a means to an end. You," he said. "Besides, I'm just a hired a hand."

The lurching form of another man darkened the doorway to the room.

"He's the one you want to register any complaints with," the militia man said, pointing back toward the man standing in the doorway.

The man entered the room, stepping into the light. Anton recognized his arrogant smirking face from his previous life. A sniveling suit, a conniving corporate weasel from Atlas who had shown interest in his work, then scoffed at one his presentations and pulled research funds away from his project.

"Getz…" Anton growled. "Where's Amanda and Sarah!"

"They are fine, I assure you. And will stay that way," Getz said. "That is, as long as you cooperate. No more savage displays of barbaric strength, please."

Anton growled under his breath. He looked into his beady eyes, glared at him, and fantasized about snapping his neck.

"You remembered me? So, all your memories and mental capacities survived the transformation. That's good to know." Getz said.

"Obviously, I was wrong about your Mesomorph project," Getz added. "Correction. My Mesomorph project. Since your work no longer officially exists. And you Dr. Mason, or at least who you used to be, has been declared missing. Or is it dead? It really doesn't matter, does it."

Getz turned to the other man.

"Now that I'm going to be the face of the company, I can't be seen with hanging around with any leaders of armed militias. You can leave now Krenshaw," Getz said. "Our business is complete and the specimen is secured."

"If you say so Getz," Krenshaw said.

Krenshaw turned back toward Anton.

"I sure wish I had someone like you in my militia," Krenshaw said.

"Once I have perfected the serum, you can have a whole army of men with his physical abilities," Getz said. "And without all the…side effects."

"We'll see," Krenshaw said turning to go.

"Oh, by the way Getz," Krenshaw added. "I was wrong about what I said before."

"Oh?" Getz said.

"The way he is looking at you…he is a killer after all," Krenshaw said. "At least when it comes to you."

"Don't worry about me," Getz said. "Because he'll be dead soon enough anyway."

Anton could hear and smell another human approaching. A female. She entered the room.

She dressed like a research scientist. Her eyes locked with Anton's. Again, it was someone Anton remembered from his past. A young hot shot scientist who wrote a few papers that he had admired.

Rachel something…Rachel Finn.

The look on her face…she was taken aback and seem surprised, if not shocked.

"What is this?" the Rachel demanded.

"What on Earth do you mean Dr, Finn?" Getz said with an annoying flair of sarcasm. "This is our specimen, of course."

"I told you that I have more than enough of his blood. Everything I need to replicate Meso48x," she said.

She pointed toward Anton and the cage.

"Why is he still here? You said he'd be released back into the Glades. And what about the woman and the girl? Are you still holding them too?" Rachel said. "This is not what we agreed to."

"What *you* agreed to Dr. Finn," Getz said. "And did you really think I was just going to get a blood sample and let him go? Just let his girlfriend and that kid go about their merry way down to the police station to file kidnapping charges?"

"I won't let you do this," Rachel said.

"Oh? So now you have a sudden ethical and moral compass" Getz said.

"And by the way, those kidnapping charges? They include you," Getz said. "Kidnapping, along with dozen other misdeeds and shortcuts you've participated in. I have it all stored in a file as thick as one of Dr. Mason's forearms there. A file I'd happy to share with the board."

Anton could see that Rachel was boiling mad and seething with frustration. But also, that Getz had the goods on her and she knew it. He owned her.

"Now, get back to work doctor, and get my damn formula ready," Getz said.

"I want to formally present some preliminary findings at the board meeting next week," he said. "Something to wet the appetite."

Anton leaned up against the steel bars of his cage, placed his hands around the steel, and squeezed as hard as he could to test the bars. He could not feel them give. Not even a little.

After a defeated Rachel walked out of the room, Getz smirked at him as if to rub Anton's face in his current predicament. A predicament that seemed so hopeless right now.

But there was a way out of any cage, and he would find it. He had to. He just had to.

It was the only way he could make sure that Amada and Sarah would be safe.

Chapter 10 – Amanda, Sarah, and Rachel

Another jet engine screamed from above causing the entire shoddy structure of the motel room to vibrate as specs of plaster and paint were shaken loose from the stained ceiling above them.

"You would think that these bigshots could have at least put up their kidnap victims in a half-decent hotel," Sarah said.

Amanda was so proud of her new friend. They had been kept prisoner in this awful room for over almost a week now, and yet Sarah had somehow managed to stay calm and maintain her warmth and quirky sense of humor.

I don't think she suspects the truth. That once Getz gets whatever he needs from Anton, he will kill him. And us too.

It was inevitable. Getz was a man obsessed with a deep-seeded greed and ruthless thirst for power that seemed to know no limits. There was no way he could afford to leave any evidence or loose ends.

Sarah must have sensed the worry overtaking Amanda. Because later in the day, after two guards delivered their evening rations, Sarah took her hand.

"It will be okay Amanda," she said reassuringly. "He will come for us. You'll see.

Rachel Finn was ashamed of herself.

She was born in the Florida panhandle and raised by a loving mother and a black Baptist preacher who instilled a strong moral center deep inside her soul. She knew right from wrong. She had always considered herself a good person. Someone who could be counted on to do the right thing.

And yet, somewhere along the way, she had allowed her frustrations to get the best of her. Frustrations the continued to build as she was passed over again and again for promotions. Bitterness that began to sour her soul as others, others being older white men, continued to take credit for her work.

That bitterness hardened into anger. Then desperation as she finally succumbed and made a deal with the devil.

The devil in the case being a relentless, charming, and shrewdly manipulative executive on the fast track named Getz. She knew exactly what he was. But she was desperate for the credit and fame that he offered. So desperate, she soon began to cross lines that her younger self, not to mention her parents, would be horrified by.

And now, thanks to her own greed and short-sightedness along with Getz's iron clad blackmail file, she really was between a rock and a hard place. To make matters worse, replicating the Mesomorph formula was proving elusive, even with the blood samples. She had isolated the rewrite chain, but all the new serum she had created from it had proven to be unstable. And with the day of the big board meeting looming, Getz was pressuring her relentlessly.

Rachel felt like she was being smothered. Her terrible choices had put her into this awful situation. Then, one day she got a wakeup call.

She walked down into the holding area on the third day of Dr. Anton Mason's captivity and witnessed the guards torching him with cattle prods "to make him docile for feeding time", she realized she no longer had a choice.

"Stop it now!" she screamed. "I need him…. undamaged. And he's half-sedated anyway you dumb fucks."

The guards tried to push back, but Rachel pushed back harder, threatening to have them fired with cause and arrested for damaging company assets.

The guards backed down, and then, she was alone with the hominid that everyone now referred to as "The Mesomorph".

He was barely conscious, reeling from the pain. His arms and torso full of cuts and wounds, a few of them on the verge of infection. She ran over to her lab to get a syringe of penicillin, a painkiller, and a first aid kit. She had the guards open up his cage to let her in. Then she told them to "leave the room…now. And don't fuck with me!"

This time the guards did not push back.

After she gave him the penicillin and the pain shot, she began to treat and bandage all his wounds. After a few minutes, he seemed to be feeling better and sat up as she put on the last of his bandages.

"Why?" he asked. "Why help?"

"I had…had to do something," she said.

"Thank you," he said.

Rachel looked into the deep luminance essence of his crayon brown eyes.

She saw and felt such a profound mixture of intelligence, tragic sadness, and pure primal beauty and innocence. He was great ape in every sense of the word. A primitive hominid possessing uncanny wisdom. The modern present merged with the ancient past. Even though he was beaten down he was still fierce and beautiful. He was remarkable.

"I…I'm sorry," she added. "I should have never agreed to help Getz."

"Amanda? Sarah?" he asked. "Where are they? Are they…"

"Yes. They are okay, For now," she said. "I overheard him talking to his guards. He is holding them at some dive motel out by the airport."

Mason tried push himself up off the concrete floor and stand upright.

"Must hurry…must save them…"

Then he collapsed back down onto the floor nearly falling back into unconscious.

"You're far too weak," she said. "You need to get your strength back first. I'll make sure the beatings stop and you get fed properly. I'll say I need you healthy for some more tests. That will give you a chance to recover,"

He nodded, sat back against the back of the cage, and took a deep breath as if to acknowledge he was taking her advice.

"And we need to come up with a plan to get you out of here," she said.

"A human disguise," he said, almost seeming to be half-joking.

Then, something occurred to her. Something major.

"Yes! That's it exactly. A human disguise," she said.

He looked at her inquisitively.

"Just sit tight and try to get your strength back," she said leaving the cage and resecuring it.

"Trust me Dr. Mason," she said. "I have an idea. I'll be back as soon as I can."

She did have an idea. It was something she had seen in the genome of Mason's blood. It was a reach. A super longshot of a crazy idea. But if she could pull it off…

Rachel trotted back down the hall to the lab and went to work.

Anton moved about the best he could inside his cage in an attempt to get some blood flowing.

At first, he was hesitant to show any signs that he was feeling more robust. But there were no cameras on the ceiling or any of the bare concrete walls, so as far as he knew, nobody was watching him when he was alone. It seemed that Getz was paranoid in his determination to keep Anton and his work a secret so that he could present the Mesomorph formula to the board as his own ingenious creation.

The past few days and nights had merged together into a hazy nightmare of physical pain combined with the horror of worry about Amanda and Sarah. But he was certain that this was his fourth day in captivity, and thanks to the kindness and courage of Rachel Finn, his wounds were healing, and he was feeling stronger by the hour.

She really was taking a big chance by trying to help him. But time was running out. Getz would soon realize she was stalling, just find another scientist to finish her work, then get rid of her along with Anton, Amanda and Sarah to destroy all the evidence.

Whatever this plan was, it needed to happen soon. Real soon.

Anton thought about Amanda and Sarah and what a brutal ordeal they were being put through. All on account of him.

If he had just killed those three pieces of shit from a distance and kept from engaging with Sarah, maybe this all could have been avoided. He felt guilty for getting Sarah involved. Sending her to Amanda with that message. He had put them both in danger. And now, he had to find a way to make things right.

He paced his cage as his anxiety escalated. He continued feeling overwhelmed by worry and guilt. It felt like time was standing still until, at last, Rachel came into the room, acting as if she was there for another round of blood samples. The guards let her in but stayed outside once the secured the door behind her. It seemed Getz's goons had no interest in being near his cage now that were forbidden to torture him for kicks.

Rachel unlocked the cage, came inside, and held up a fat syringe with a golden liquid inside it.

She smiled.

"Good news?" Anton asked.

"Yes…but with an asterisk," she said.

"Recreating your formula is proving to be a bitch and quite frankly I don't think no one will be able to do it without your original notes, none of which have been recovered," she said.

"Good," he said. "Humans cannot be trusted with something…that powerful. The formula will die with me."

"Recreating it might be impossible. But, reversing it, not so much," she said.

Anton nearly fell over in shock and delight.

"What? Did you…really?"

"Yes. Only in a test tube of course, but like I said, there is a catch," she said.

"Yes?" Anton asked.

"The genetic rewrites you created are too strong. Too permanent in your genome at this point," she said. "This counter agent may have worked as a permanent reversal agent right after you first took the Mesomorph formula. But now…it's temporary. And Anton, it's a one-time deal."

"How much time will I have?" he asked.

"Ninety minutes," she said. "Maybe two hours tops."

Anton stayed silent for a moment taking in the enormous impact of everything she had just said.

"That's enough time to me out of here," he said. "And get out to that motel."

"Exactly what I was thinking," she said.

"Now remember, it will be easy to sneak you out of here. I can put a lab coat on you and dress you up like one of my assistants," she said. "But you won't have any super strength to deal with the guards."

"Can we use something in that medical bag to knock them out?" he asked.

She opened the bag and pulled out four fully loaded syringes with nice long needles.

Anton grunted and nodded with delight

"I told you I had a plan," Rachel smiled.

She held up the syringe with the counter agent and tapped it to get rid of the air bubbled

Anton stared up into golden amber. A golden amber that would make him human again, at least for a while.

"Do it," he said.

Chapter 11 – Airport Rescue

It was bizarre transforming back into a modern say Homo sapien.

It was the exact opposite of the experience he had gone through de-evolving into a primitive hominid. It was almost instant, and he hardly felt a single sensation. Except for one thing.

Without his physical strength and lighting quick reflexes and agility, he felt extremely vulnerable. Thank God for Rachel and her medical back loaded up with syringes full of knock-out cocktails and tranquilizer darts. They took two of the guards' rifles and one of the handguns. But Anton cautioned not to use them unless absolutely necessary.

"I'm already leaving you with a hell of mess to clean up," Anton said. "Let's try not add any dead bodies to it."

"I feel you," Rachel said. "Not looking to add murder to the rap sheet."

Once they had put all the guards in their path to sleep, thanks to his new, temporary human form and the official Atlas lab coat and badge, leaving the facility was without incident. They simply walked down to the parking lot, got into Rachel's SUV, navigated through the mid-day Miami traffic until they were headed north on I-95 and on their way to the hotel room

"I'm really appreciate what you are doing here Rachel," he said. "I'm so sorry about the price you will pay."

"Hey, I deserve it. I did the crime I'll do the time," she said. "But I will take satisfaction…great satisfaction, that Getz will be there behind bars right with me, and hopefully for a lot longer. I have an entire phone, make those two phones, full of enough shit to put that bastard away for life."

After about twenty minutes of driving on I-836, Rachel took an exit that leading to a small corporate park that was smack up against the airport. Then she took them down a street with liquor stores and pawn shops until they reached a rundown motel.

"Here we go," she said.

Rachel looked at her watch.

"We need to move fast," she said. "You are running out of time."

"I'll cover the guards with the rifle while you do your thing with the shots," he said. "No worries. We'll be in and out, hopefully without having to shoot anybody."

Living life trapped as a prisoner in some shady motel room was torture.

Maybe not physical torture in the sense that nobody was waterboarding or taking a blowtorch to them. But for Amanda, they may as well have been.

This was emotional, mental, psychological torture. Between the nonstop paint chipping, plaster busting roars of the jet engines zooming a mere couple hundred feet about their heads, combined with the not knowing where Anton was or even if he was alive or when and how they planned to kill her and Sarah, it was enough the make even the strongest, most confident mind begin to break after several days.

Sarah had been remarkably brave. So much so that she was inspiring Amanda to stay strong. But still, they were running out of time.

One day, there was a commotion outside the door. Amanda was sure that this was it. The day they were both going to die.

The commotion outside the door grew louder. She heard a body crash to the floor. Then she heard someone shouting, "drop your weapon. Now!"

The voice was impossibly familiar.

No. It could not be.

· Then the door to the motel room opened and Amanda saw with her very own eyes that the impossible had become real.

It was Anton. Anton in his human form.

An eternal moment of transcendent joy passed between them as they looked at each other. Before Amanda could say his name, Sarah beat her to the punch.

"Anton!" Sarah said, running up to hug him. "I knew you'd come for us. I just knew it."

"Sarah," he said. "But how did you know it was me?"

"Your eyes," Sarah said, smiling.

"The window to the soul," Rachel added.

Amanda gave Rachel a look that said, *what the hell is she doing here?*

"It's okay, she's with us," Anton said. "She helped me escape. And gave me this form back. But it's only temporary."

"Temporary?" Amanda said. "How long?"

Anton looked toward Rachel who checked her watch.

"We've got an hour tops," Rachel said. "We need to get out to I-75 near the Glades before you begin to change back."

"Let's move," Anton said, guiding Sarah and Amanda out of the room and down the hall to the stairwell as they followed Rachel.

When they reached the bottom of the stairwell. Anton stopped and took Amanda's hand.

"Rachel, take Sarah with you and go get the car," he said. "We'll out back in a minute."

Rachel nodded, giving them a thumbs up. It seemed she understood that Amanda and Anton needed a moment alone. And it was a moment that Amanda did not want to waste.

She wrapped her arms around him and kissed him. A warm, wet, desperate, heart-aching kiss that spoke of how horribly she had missed him and how empty it had been without him.

"I can't imagine how awful it's been for you," she said. "How lonely."

"It was the dream that this moment might be possible…that is what kept me going," Anton said.

"Maybe there's a way to make this permanent," Amanda said. "Or at least, have more moments like this?"

Anton looked down and shook his head.

"The DNA code receptors will fuse shut after I revert back," he said. "This is a one-time thing."

"We'll find a way Anton. A way to be together, even if it's in your primitive form," she said. "I'll never give up. Never."

She could hear a car engine rumble up to the exit door.

They looked into each other's eyes one more time, knowing it could be the last, then popped the door open and hopped into the back seat of the SUV, with Rachel driving and Sarah in the front passenger seat.

Sarah made a quick call to her parents to let them know that she was alive and okay. The call did not go so well, but Sarah handled it with such calm and poise. She really was a remarkable young woman.

"Mom, it's all good, I swear. Better than good," Sarah said into the phone. "I'll explain it all when I get home…yes, in about an hour."

"Explain it all?" Rachel asked.

"Well, maybe not quite all," Sarah said.

Rachel drove with a sense of urgency and purpose but was careful not to go enough past the speed limit to risk a pullover.

A tense half forty-five minutes of so passed and so far, so good. Nobody was following them. Then when they at last reached an exit for the recreational area of the Big Cypress National Park. Amanda felt a sense of relief that they had made it safely. But also, a foreboding sense of dread.

It was time to say good-bye again and this time it was going to hurt even more.

There were a handful of people in the recreational area, unhitching boats, preparing to fish, setting up for picnic lunches. Amanda noticed Rachel looking at her watch with worry while trying to hurry everyone along down the hiking trail. Rachel led the way followed by Sarah, with Anton and Amanda walking briskly hand in hand to bring up the rear.

Amanda heard a beeping go off and saw Rachel look at her watch again.

"We're overdue now," Rachel warned. "Let's hope we are far enough into the woods because it's going to happen any second now."

And then, at the exact moment that Amanda squeezed his right hand, it happened.

She felt his hand swell up, his palm widened, his fingers grew long and thick, as the soft fleshy hands of a scientist became coarse and strong to the touch.

She watched as Anton's torso expanded, his chest muscles thickened, his back became wide, his arms, long, sinewy, and heavily muscles. He became hirsute, covered with a beautiful sheen of dark hair speckled generous tuffs of silver.

His face transformed right before her eyes; from the handsome human she had fallen into love with to something retro human. Something primitive and yet so aching beautiful.

Then there were his eyes. The very same eyes. The very same soul. And when she looked at him, she fell in love all over again.

"Dr. Mason…. Amanda…"

The sound of Rachel's voice cut through the thick blanket bittersweet emotion Amanda was feeling.

"I'm sorry to interrupt, but we need to make this fast," Rachel said. "If someone were to come up the trail…"

"I understand," Anton said.

"Dr. Finn…Rachel," Anton said. "Thank you for everything."

"It was the least I could do," Rachel said.

And with that, Amanda and embraced, an embrace of love that spanned across the eons of time and evolution. She could manage no words. It was just too painful. She just watched him, relishing the sight, while backing up to let the others say goodbye.

"Dr. Finn…Rachel," Anton said. "Thank you for everything."

"It was the least I could do," Rachel said.

Sarah stood before Anton, hesitating. Amanda could tell it was killing the poor girl to have to say goodbye to this extraordinary new friend.

Sarah ran up and held onto Anton, crying into his shoulder.

"You made it possible for me to see Amanda again. You made my dream come true," Anton said. "Thank you."

"I'll never forget you," Sarah said.

The four of them stood there for second, savoring one last moment together.

Then, as the sound of hikers approached, Anton gave Amanda one last heartbreaking look, then drifted back into the dense foliage and disappeared into the forest.

Bonus Origin Story

"The Mesomorph"

The Mesomorph

The Mesomorph

James J. Caterino

Chapter 1 – Saturday Night Blues

Doctor Anton Mason used every spec of his considerable brainpower to stay focused on his work. But the relentless pounding of the obnoxious music was too much to take.

The putrid notes merged together with the grating screams emanating from the patio full of drunken assholes fusing into a raging cacophony—a cocktail of bursting decibels that made any form of rational thought impossible.

This is fucking insane, he thought.

Not even his idols, James Watson or Albert Einstein, could have concentrated under such circumstances. Nor Leonardo da Vinci, Sir Isaac Newton, Plato, or Aristotle himself for that matter.

None of them ever had to endure the nonstop stress and anxiety of living next door to Johnny Bluto, an adult version of the neighborhood bully from your childhood nightmares, the date rapist fraternity slob from your college, and the over-bearing dickhead sales guy from the office—all merged into one beer-guzzling, property line ignoring, toxic human.

And the tragedy of it all, Johnny Bluto was, by all of society's standards, quite successful.

Like the cult leader politician who said, and rightly so, that he will be winning so much, you would be sick of him winning, Johnny Bluto kept being rewarded for his repugnant behavior. He had a wickedly hot wife half his age, and more friends than Anton had even had if you counted up everyone he had ever had a conversation with since the kindergarten. And as far as Anton could tell, seemed to be an immense financial success as a result of some sort of sales.

Of course, since the city did have an actual strongly-worded noise and disturbing the peace ordinance, that should, in theory, make that kind of raging frat house parties Bluto had almost nightly impossible. So, you would think Anton could just call the police and that would be the end of it. But the keyword here is theory.

Anton had tried calling the cops twice before. The first time, they never came.

So, during the next night of festivities, he thought he would try to reason with Bluto. You know, walk over and nicely ask if they could turn down the music a bit.

Bluto turned a hose on him. Literally.

As Anton stood there feeling weak, naked, and vulnerable in front of the patio full of drunken fiends, like he was once again a twelve-year-old kid terrified of the school bullies lurking around the corner, Bluto turned a hose on him—fully cranked at the jet spray setting.

It was the most humiliating moment of Anton Mason's life, and being smart, and geeky, and science obsessed and a bit anti-social, he had experienced plenty of them.

So the following time, when the middle-age partiers held their next fraternity style multi-kegger, he tried calling the police yet again.

This time they actually did come.

The cops must have told Bluto and company to chill because, for the rest of that night, things went quiet. But then, for the next several months, Anton experienced the wrath of the vindictive, bulling Bluto on a daily basis. Everything from flat tires on his car, to birthday party bounce house in his backyard with about a hundred screaming brats.

After that, Anton just gave up.

The stress of the daily battle with Bluto had exhausted him, and the man seemed to have an endless appetite for neighborhood warfare and boundless energy to attack whomever he deemed an enemy, and right now, that was Anton Mason.

So now, when he worked from home at night, as he did pretty much every night, Mason just put on headsets and turned up the volume to try and drown out the middle-age drunken scumbags next door.

But it was no use.

Breaking down the evolutionary sequences in the human genome and backtracking the historical records of the mutations within—that was his work. And it took an intensity of focus and concentration that few humans were capable of, and Anton could sense he was getting close to figuring it all out. How to unlock the secrets of the human past, to create a therapy for the present and future. How to turn back the biological clock and push back against every aging disease and condition there was.

As the ear-splitting party next door raged on, he took off the headset, gathered up his notes and laptop, and headed downtown to the lab. He would have to stay there for the night, and maybe even the weekend—again.

But soon, it would all be worth it, he told himself. A major breakthrough was coming. It was right around the corner.

He could feel it in his bones.

Later that night at the lab, Anton did his nightly shutdown routine where he went through his old-school hand-written notebook and added updates to the charts and diagrams that he had drawn to map out the evolutionary history of the human genome and all of the mitochondrial mutations that had taken place since the genetic split between humans and chimpanzees from a common ancestor some 4.6 million years ago.

Then, as often happened on these late nights, he came across one of his sketches of Amanda.

He put the pencil to it and began to feel better already.

He began to add more shading into the shimmering highlights of her hair and put more details onto the exquisite lips. He added a touch of expression to her captivating gaze, the gaze that made him melt every time he made eye contact with her at the lab.

Such encounters were always the highlight of his day.

Amanda Zakori.

A while back, he had been all set to resign from the lab and return to teaching when he heard that Amanda was coming to work there. Of course, he immediately tore up his resignation letter and stayed just to be around her.

He had a crush on her since he was the age when people started having crushes, which for him was the sixth grade.

Amanda was the lost love that never was. The girl he had admired from afar forever, never having the courage to approach her about those feelings and endure the inevitable cruelty of the rejection that would come his way. Even now, when she was currently single, that was a barrier he dared not cross.

Because that rejection would be final. The end.

At least now, there was a comfort in the possibility. There was a chance, if only in his over-active imagination.

Anton put down the notebook, slumped back into the stiff vinyl upholstery of the office chair, and soon, he was dreaming of molecular mutations, the human genome, and a life with Amanda Zakori.

Chapter 2 – Office Politics

Anton walked into the lecture hall with a knot of anxiety deep in his gut.

He hated these events because this was not a lecture at all. If that were the case, he'd be tickled pink to talk all day about his theories to a group of eager undergrad Anthropology or Biology students. But no, this was not a lecture at all.

It was a sales pitch.

Anton was a salaried employee of the HUBRC, the Harbor University Biology Research Center in Coral Gables, Florida. But all of his research funding, and indeed all of HUBRC's economic well-being, was dependent on money from the pharmaceutical industry.

So today, he would not be addressing eager future scientists of college age or even angst-ridden pimply-faced teens like the ones he once taught when he was a Dade County High School biology teacher. Today, he would be trying to sell his life-long work to a room full of fat-cat executives from Big Pharma. A group of men and women who were motivated by one thing and one only— greed.

You know what? That's fine, he told himself, taking a deep breath before stepping up to the podium as the slide show presentation began behind him.

Because I got the angle, even you greedy bastards can't say no to.

"Good afternoon," Anton said, "I am Dr. Anton Mason, the head of anti-aging and disease preventive research at HUBRC, and thank you for coming."

He stared out at a group of glassy-eyed, disconnected, apathetic suits, most of whom were staring at their phones and ignoring the meticulous presentation booklets he had so carefully prepared and placed on their seats.

The slide show presentation behind him flashed a series of older, frail people scored to sad, mournful music, followed by shots of young, vibrant, super-fit people set to a triumphant fanfare.

Anton began his presentation.

"The fountain of youth," he said. "Finding it has been and still is the eternal quest of the human species."

He let his opening statement sink in a bit. A few people seemed to wake up and were listening to him. But still, as one yawing prick confirmed, this was a tough room.

"What causes aging? What, for lack of a better word, makes people old? Is it wrinkled skin, or gray hair, or fading eyesight? Well, those can all be corrected, to a certain extent, right?"

He continued.

"Botox, plastic surgery, or even a good skincare routine for the wrinkles. A dye job for the hair, or a piece if you've gone bald. And glasses, contacts, or Lasix surgery for the eyes. But here's the rub. Those are not the causes of aging. Those are the symptoms. The cause of aging? The breakdown of the system at the neural, endocrine, and cellular level."

"But here is the good news. The breakthrough," he added. "We can control it. And—as I will show you—even reverse it."

Anton walked over to the laptop on a nearby table and manually changed the slide to reveal a series of images of before and after images of older people. In the before pictures, they looked pathetic—frail, weak, old. In the after pictures, they looked astonishingly better. Standing more erect. Dramatically improved muscle tone. More color and even better skin with far fewer wrinkles.

Most of the room was looking at him now.

He was speaking their language. These greedy bastards knew this was something they could sell.

"To achieve the changes you see in these slides, there was no plastic surgery, hair dye, miracle snake oil rejuvenation cream, or bad toupees employed."

"Then how?" a ruddy-faced, old, chubby salesman from the audience barked out.

"This was a case where the scientific and medical community took its cue from ongoing anecdotal research happening in the public since the 1960s," Anton replied. "An explosion taking place in the gyms, training rooms, and practice fields around the world, namely performance-enhancing drugs. Some of which you people manufacture."

"So, they're juiced up," some young thick-necked man called out. Someone who looked as if he might have partaken in some of those pharmaceuticals.

"In a manner of speaking, yes," Anton said. "They are on testosterone and HGH, human growth hormone. But at clinical replacement dosages, a far less amount and without all the other synthetic androgens and countless non-steroidal agents that a competitive athlete would use such as insulin, thermogenics, and amphetamines. This brings the side effects down to a negligible level."

"And they don't just look better and feel better," Anton continued. "They are healthier across the board, both physically, mentally, and even emotionally. Improved bone density, better lipid profiles, lower blood pressure, improved reaction times, and intelligence. Deeper, better sleep—and better sex. Yeah, you heard me."

The audience chuckled. Finally, he had them.

Except for that one interrupting loudmouth. The chubby ruddy-faced guy.

"Yeah, but so what. We know all this, and this stuff has been practiced now since the early 2000s," the chubby guy scoffed. "So why am I here? Or are you wasting our time?"

What a fucking asshole.

Anton fought the overwhelming feeling of being flustered. Even here, in this sacred space, he had to deal with bullying blowhards.

"I'm getting to that, sir," Anton said.

He gathered himself as he walked over to the laptop. He changed the slide presentation, and a human evolutionary tree appeared.

"As nice as the prior examples are, that is not true anti-aging, merely improved quality of life," Anton said. "But what if we could have both? And what if it was permanent? No long-term regimen of daily and weekly injections. Just one short therapy— just one, cycle, if you will."

He went on. At this point, it did not even matter if the audience was there. This was his passion. Anton was in his zone.

"There was a time in the past when we were stronger, faster, more resistant to disease, and in all the ways that really matter, actually smarter. That is because we had to be. We kept our bone density and muscle mass without any chemical assistance. We had primal sex up until the day we died. And we never had to worry about crow's feet or losing our hair. Our prehistoric ancestors, the hominids from which we were spawned—they were, in every sense of the word, a physically superior species."

"Now the question is," he added. "How do we get that back?"

He pointed to the screen.

"The key to creating a longer and better future is unlocking the past, and we now know how to do that by looking inside the human genome, which is an evolutionary time capsule. Every mutation, every change. It's all in there with the same exact precision as digital data is stored on a hard drive."

Anton looked out at the audience. Once again, they were with him.

"Please open the presentation booklet I left on your seat," he said. "And I will walk you through the science. And show you all the practical and world-changing implications of the new formula I am working on here at HUBRC."

"Mason, you blew them away. It was a smashing success," Roberts said. "I have four offers to fund the research in return for the initial rights. It's a bidding war. Good job, pal."

Roberts was his boss.

Anton had no feelings about him one way or another. He was just a typical corporate stooge.

But he was being way too nice. Sure, Anton was happy about the success of the pitch, and he really did appreciate Roberts giving him some props. But still, something was off.

"So now that you scored on this one for us, I want to move you over to the energy team to…"

Here it was.

The big slap down Roberts had been buttering him up for.

He did not even hear the rest of what his boss said. All he knew was that something he created was being taken from him. And to add to the punch in the gut, moving to the energy team meant being at a different facility—and away from Amanda.

"But this is my project," Anton said.

Roberts' expression instantly morphed from the fake warm salesman to one of an ice-cold, ruthless dictator boss.

"Actually, Dr. Mason, you're wrong. It belongs to HUBRC. It says so right there in your employee contract," Roberts said with smug satisfaction.

"But I've worked on this formula my whole career. Even back in college. It was my doctorate thesis," Anton said. "It's my formula."

"Again, no, it's not. And if you want to take up with legal, be my guest. But they will tell you the same thing," Roberts said.

"And I'd appreciate it if you could update Lee Colt and his team before you move over to Energy," Roberts added. "He'll be taking over the project from here."

This just kept getting worse.

Lee Colt was Roberts' golf buddy. A smarmy dickhead who was always ogling and hitting on Amanda. He was an ass hat of the first order.

Anton wanted to scream. He wanted to rage and break something—or better yet—someone. But instead, he walked away and hurried back to his lab.

He was going to protect his formula one way or another.

63

Chapter 3 – The Formula

Anton spun the combination lock and looked into the facial recognition camera. A second later, the refrigerator door clicked open.

This was the unit he kept in his office away from the main lab, to keep an eye on samples he wanted to monitor around the clock without jumping through all the hoops required for entry into the main lab's cooler.

Roberts had grudgingly approved his request for this personal fridge in his office. But what neither Roberts nor anyone else knew was what Anton had stored inside it.

He pulled out a case of glass ampules, held them up to the light, and gazed wantonly at the golden liquid inside.

This was it—his life's work.

This was the prototype for the formula. His formula. And he was not about to let Roberts or anyone else take it away from him.

Thanks to his cut-throat boss, the process had to be accelerated, and it was now time to begin human trials on a volunteer human subject—himself.

He took out one of the golden ampules, reached into a first aid kit for a 22-gauge needle with a three-cc syringe. Then he withdrew the golden liquid into the syringe, swapped out the needles, grabbed an alcohol pad, and prepared to give himself an intermuscular injection into the upper outside quadrant of his right glute.

He found a spot, poked the needle in deep, and pressed down on the plunger.

There was a knock at his door.

"Anton, are you in there?"

He would know that soothing, angelic voice anywhere.

It was Amanda.

He frantically mopped the injection site with an alcohol pad, pulled up his pants, tossed the used syringe into a medical waste can and slid the case of vials back into the fridge.

Just in time.

The door began to open as Anton scrambled to gather himself, answer, and get seated behind his desk.

"Yeah, sure," he said. "Sorry, I was…deep in thought."

As with everything that seemed to come out of his mouth around Amanda, it felt so awkward and lame.

"I understand. It must be how you come up with all this crazy stuff," she said. "Stuff no one else is capable of thinking up."

There was an awkward moment of silence between them. But it was different this time than normal. Anton felt like it was a good awkwardness —that she was somehow looking at him differently now.

"I heard about your presentation," she said. "And I heard you knocked it out of the part."

Anton felt himself blush.

"That's awesome," Amanda said.

"Congratulations," she added after another moment of awkward silence.

"Thank you, Amanda," he said. "Thank you for saying that."

"Well, you deserved it," she said. "But what you do not deserve is what Roberts did to you. That's so bush league. He should not be in that job. He's not even a scientist. Just some hack Big Pharma wanted in there."

Anton nodded and shrugged his shoulders in a "yeah, I know, but what can I do?" gesture.

Amanda's phone chimed from an incoming text.

"Sorry, I gotta run," she said. "Meeting some people for lunch."

"I understand," he said. "Have fun."

She paused for a moment as if contemplating something.

"Hey, would you like to come?" she asked. "It's a big group of us heading down to the Cheese Factory."

Big group translated into there would be some people there whom Anton couldn't take, including that project thief and office blowhard Lee Colt. The perverted prick would not miss out on the chance to ogle and harass Amanda.

"I really can't. I have so much work to do. Getting the new team up to speed and all," he said. "But I appreciate the offer. And I really appreciate you coming by here like this, Amanda. I…really do."

She smiled at him in a way that seemed to radiate deep into the depths of his flesh. It made him feel so alive.

Was he over reading her and over feeling things?

Or maybe the formula was working on him much faster than anticipated. The models showed one week to ten days to begin feeling the effects. But this formula was a spike forward into new, unexplored territory. So much was unknown about gene-altering therapies such as this. He was literally rewriting his DNA.

"Maybe some other time?" she said.

"Yes. I would like that," he said. "I would like that very much."

She smiled again and turned to leave.

"See you around then," she said at the door.

"Yes, see you around," he said.

And with that, Amanda disappeared, and Anton went about securing the rest of the formula into his briefcase.

There would be a boosting dose in two days, followed by six weekly injections. And then it would all be done. The DNA would be re-written. The effects would be full-blown, cemented in at the genetic level, and permanent.

Anton felt a rush inside, a surge of adrenaline in anticipation of what was about to happen.

Nobody could ever take his work from him again because his physical form, his flesh, his very physical essence—that would be the proof and the embodiment of everything he had worked for through all these years.

Chapter 4 – The Transformation

The next three days passed by more or less according to the daily established rhythms of his normal life.

Anton, as always, swallowed his anger, went to work, and dutifully handed over materials to the Lee Colt team. He took some satisfaction over the fact that their dipshit leader was clueless, and neither he nor his team would be able to grasp any of Anton's notes anyway.

He saw Amanda a few times, and there was the glancing smile and hello. Anton wanted so bad to follow up on the encounter from his office the other day by asking her to lunch, or God forbid dinner. But, as always, he lacked the courage.

His nights at home remained the same with non-stop raging beer parties next door as he tried in vain to battle the cacophony of obnoxiousness by keeping his headsets cranked up while listening to John Williams' soundtracks.

Three days and nothing had changed.

He felt no different. Looked no different. Even after he injected his upper outside left glute with the follow-up booster dose. He was beginning to wonder if the formula was a bust. If maybe the instruction codes were not able to penetrate his DNA to apply and reverse all of the historical evolutionary mutations.

He was beginning to get depressed.

But then, on the morning of the fifth day, something happened.

It started with the way he woke up. Or rather, what part of him that woke up first. It was as if his covers were being propped up by a steel beam. It was something that hadn't happened in more years than he cared to remember. He felt like a teenager, and it felt good.

When he got out of bed, he did so with pleasant ease.

The bad back, the creaking knees, the stiff neck and shoulders, the pain in the feet—all of the aches of pains of his under-exercised forty-two-year-old body were now gone. Vanished. Even his eyesight was improved. As a matter of fact, it was perfect. He felt no need to put his glasses on.

Even the way he moved when he walked down into the kitchen was different. And he had the sudden urge to move some more.

He downed a quick cup of coffee and dug through the closet for his fancy Brooks running shoes. He dusted off the cobwebs. It had been that long.

He had bought them to begin a walking program, figuring he could walk at night while listening to audiotapes of his favorite science lectures. But somehow, the program never happened because every time he tried to walk, everything ached.

But this time, it was different.

Anton put on a pair of shorts and a t-shirt, laced up the Brooks, and headed out the front door. Not on a walk—but a run.

There was a spring in his step that had never been there before. He felt oddly bouncy, liked he had wind-up springs in his legs. He seemed to be able to take in big lungful of air in a way he never could before.

And he could now run. Really run. Run with ease and authority.

He felt so loose and fast.

He ran up the street, taking long, springy strides.

He turned the corner and ran down the next street, ramping up his velocity, faster and faster.

He weaved in and out of walkers and joggers and people on bikes, blowing by them all with such graceful ease.

He leaped over a bush, hurdled a four-foot-high fence, and sprinted down an asphalt trail through a park, then back out into the neighborhood again.

He ran until he couldn't run anymore and good God, it felt fantastic.

When he returned home, he was famished. Hungry in a way he had never been before, at least not as an adult. He proceeded to eat an entire box of granola with a bucket of blueberries and washed it all down with almost an entire half-gallon carton of milk.

Something was happening all right.

Something big.

Now it was time for further experimentation. So when his breakfast digested, Anton decided to make his debut at the local Gold's Gym.

He had tried going to the gym before. A long time ago, when he was still in his late teens. And he was, if nothing else, dedicated. He diligently performed the routines listed in the magazines, always ate six times a day, and even chugged down protein shakes. But little happened.

"You're an ectomorph," the gym owner said to him while gazing at Anton with the pity most people would reserve for someone, say, terminally ill.

"But there is one last resort that might help," he said, handing him a pharmaceutical bottle containing one hundred tiny blue pills.

The label read "Dianabol."

The gym owner prescribed three tablets a day.

And they did help. At least at first. A little bit anyway. He gained about seven pounds, felt a bit stronger. But then the pills stopped working. Worse, he lost what little gains he made.

"Your system's shutting down," the gym owner said. "You need to get off and train natural for a while."

But then what? Should he try again?

"Kid, I'll be straight with you," he said. "You'd be wasting your time. You just don't have the genetics for this. Ectos like you are more suited to cross country running and stuff like that."

There was that word. Genetics. What the gym owner was talking about, in gym speak, was the three broad categories of body types—ectomorphs, endomorphs, and mesomorphs.

Ectomorphs like Anton were slight of build, perhaps even frail, and did not put on muscle very easily if at all. Endomorphs were round in shape, usually soft with a lot of body fat and no muscularity. Mesomorphs, now that was where you wanted to be. Strong, muscular, with low levels of body fat, and a gifted nervous system and metabolism. Think NFL running back or Olympic sprinter.

Yeah, maybe I used to be an ectomorph. But now, thanks to the formula, I might just be the most genetically gifted mesomorph on the planet.

He could not wait to get to the gym.

The gym was packed with massive meatheads and beautifully buff fitness chicks that looked so perfect; Anton wondered if they were using some kind of formula of their own.

The old Anton would have been absolutely terrified in a place like this. But now—now that he had an endocrine system pumping out enough testosterone and growth hormone and a fully wired nervous system, he could actually benefit from this place.

Pumping and primping. Expending so much time and energy, repeatedly lifting the same piece of iron over and over again. Before, it had seemed like such a pointless waste of time and energy to him. But now, he was anxious to see what the fuss was all about.

After a brief warm-up of calisthenics in the stretching area, Anton walked over to a pull-up bar mounted up high on the wall. He remembered from his past gym experience that nobody ever used it, preferring to do the "assisted chins" on a machine that helped push you up from the bottom. It seemed that it was still the case today. The area around the pull-up bar was desolate. The reason was simple. Most people, even in this hard-core gym, could actually do un-assisted pull-ups, at least not for very many reps and not without kicking and bucking like a bronco at a rodeo show.

But Anton found no such difficulty. He held his body perfectly straight up and down, pulled up until his upper chest smacked the bar, and held the position for several seconds. Then he lowered himself down into the fully hanging position and hoisted himself back up in the same exact manner—twenty times.

He repeated the same set again, but with a forty-five-pound plate strapped to a belt around his waist. Then a set with two forty-five-pound plates. In between those sets, instead of resting, he dropped to the ground and did push-ups—fifty at a time.

He began to feel the mythical "pump." His muscles seemed to swell to gargantuan levels as a network of engorged veins sprouted up and seemed to pop out of his shoulders and arms.

For the first time in his life, Anton Mason was buff

Now, Anton understood the pump. It felt amazing. Like a never-ending blissful orgasm of flesh and blood.

The muscular meatheads and drop-dead gorgeous fitness babes who before would have ignored or even mocked him, stared at him with respect, even awe. A few of them, from both sexes, even eyed him up lustfully.

Everything was changing. Anton knew that from this moment forward, things were going to different.

Very different.

Chapter 5 – New Attitude

It was Friday, and today would be the day.

Today would be the day he crossed that seemingly impenetrable barrier and asked Amanda out. And the thing is, he wasn't even nervous. Not really. Just excited.

The effects of the formula re-writing his genetic code was not just physical. It wasn't just the veiny arms of a bodybuilder or the speed of an Olympic sprinter. It was mental and emotional, as well. For the first time in his life, Dr. Anton Mason was confident. Not just the normal type self-confidence. This was more like NFL quarterback, fighter pilot self-confidence.

So, when Amanda stepped into the elevator with him, Anton saw the opening, and he ran with it.

She smiled and said, "hello." He did the same, pressing the button for the third floor. But his eyes were not on the elevator panel. His gaze was fixed upon Amanda.

The way she was looking at him—it was the same way as in his office that time she had stopped by. Back then, he thought he sensed something. Now, he was sure of it. He could feel the electric pull between them—the chemistry—the primal magnetism.

"Amanda, I was wondering if maybe we could get together after work," he said, with a quiet confidence that now seemed so natural to him.

"Oh?" she said, seeming quite surprised, but in a good way. At least he hoped.

"Yeah, for dinner," he said. "And maybe a movie afterward. It'd Flashback Friday down at the Showcase Cinema in the Grove, and they're showing *Back to the Future*. I mean, if you're into that kinda thing."

"I absolutely adore *Back to the Future*," she said. "And I like eating too."

"So?" he asked

"So, yes," she said. "Of course, Anton. I'd love to."

It was all happening so fast, and it all seemed so surreal.

Anton had to focus on keeping from bursting into song and dance at the realization that the moment he rehearsed and dreamt of his entire life was happening—right now.

The elevator doors opened. As they both turned to the right, they were looking at each other, still engaged in the breakthrough conversation.

"Fantastic!" Anton said. "Just text me so I have your number and I'll get back to you with all the details and time when…"

Then, the moment of blissful euphoria came crashing down like he had been hit by a sledgehammer.

Lee Colt was walking down the hall.

Straight toward them.

Literally splitting the two of them like a running back splitting defender.

The interrupting prick swung his back to Anton as if casting him aside like some sort of irrelevant insect and began talking to Amanda while lurching into her personal space.

"Hey, I been looking for you," he said. "A bunch of us are going to Happy Hour and…"

Enough!

Before, he would feel nothing but humiliation when something like this happened. Then he would shut down and spend days feeling weak and depressed.

But now he felt only a cascading rage.

A primal, savage, primitive rage.

Despite that, Anton tried. He really, really tried to be civil. To take that high road.

"Excuse me," he said, in the most polite tone he could as the barbaric volcano percolated inside him.

Lee Colt ignored him and kept jabbering his rap to Amanda as if he were God's gift to women.

"Excuse me," Anton repeated, this time tapping him on the shoulder. "We were in the middle of a conversation here."

Lee Colt did acknowledge him. He swung around and glared at Anton. Then the glare gave way to a mocking, dismissive smirk.

"Yeah, I do mind," Lee Colt said. "Beat it, Mason. Go back into your lab and get to work on those transition reports for me."

Anton could no longer contain the simmering savagery boiling inside him.

He snapped his left hand forward with the lighting speed of a professional boxer, took a vice grip on Lee Colt's neck, and lifted him off the ground. In the same blur of continuous motion, he drove his enemy straight back up against the wall.

Then, he just held him there, relishing the fear he could smell oozing from every foul-smelling pore on Lee Colt's pale skin.

And he could really smell him. All of his senses were now several times sharper than before. Especially smell and hearing. As he held Lee Colt up in the air, pinning against the wall with a squeezing grip around his neck, he could literally hear the pulsating carotid artery of his conquered foe.

Anton could feel the spike of strength all throughout his body and especially in the left arm and hand that had neutralized the bullying, office loudmouth named Lee Colt.

Anton knew he could make it, so Lee Colt never bothered anyone else again. He could crush his throat and snap his neck with one squeeze of the vice-grip strength he now possessed in his hand.

But He did not want to kill Lee Colt. Not really. He just wanted to teach him a lesson. And as Anton's super sharp hearing picked up the gasping breaths amid the otherwise dead silence around him, it was clear that he had an audience.

Lee Colt was being humiliated in front of his peers.

Anton tossed him aside like a rag doll and watched him roll across the floor.

"Don't you ever, ever, EVER interrupt me again," Anton roared. "You understand me, tough guy?"

His fallen quarry was too shocked and terrified to answer.

Anton kept his eyes firmly locked onto Lee Colt, wishing so bad the project-stealing dick head would take a run and maybe a swing at him. But alas, all the pitiful prick could barely manage to do was pick himself up off the floor and scurry away like a frightened rat.

Off to file a complaint at human resources, no doubt.

So be it, Anton thought. He was done with this place anyway. He already had the only thing he wanted from this office. A chance with Amanda. His lifelong fantasy. And now he had it.

Or did he?

He prayed that in this exercise to finally assert himself, he did not scare off the one true thing he had always longed for.

Chapter 6 – Date With an Angel

"Well, that thing in the office today. Yeah, that was tense. And it was a little too much testosterone for me,' Amanda said. "But, can I be totally honest with you?"

They had just seen *Back to the Future* and were now at dinner, splitting a large thin crust vegan pizza and a salad for two at Mama Luciani's in the Grove. She had picked the place and the dish, and for Anton, the dream date was going exactly how he had imagined it. But better, because it was so real. Almost hyper-real like everything was to him in his new, finely-tuned, enhanced state.

"Of course," Anton answered. "From all the time I have known you, going back to the sixth grade, you've never been one to hold back, so don't do it now."

She smiled and even laughed a bit, seeming impressed that he had taken notice of such detail about her.

"Well, yeah, I get that from my mother," she said.

"I remember her," he said. "She was a great lady. And a very beautiful woman…like her daughter."

"Why, thank you," she said with a slight blush.

There was a moment between them. Anton could feel the connection. It was physical. And it was emotional. Halfway through one date and he was as certain as ever that he was with the woman of his dreams.

"So anyway—the tell it like it is thing. Shoot," he said.

"Okay," she said.

"Well, here's the thing. I don't want to condone violence or anything," she said. "But I've known you since the sixth grade also and noticed something about you. Something that always frustrated me."

"Oh?" Anton said, shocked and happy that she had ever noticed anything about him, even if it was negative.

"You were always such a nice guy," she said. "But too nice. You let people push you around. And quite frankly, I was happy…hell, I was downright static to see you push back."

She looked at him in a deep, searing way. A wanting, primal, physical, lustful way.

"And he is such an asshole," she added. "If anybody needed an ass-kicking, it was Lee Colt."

"He had it coming," Anton said. "Kind of like Biff in *Back to Future*."

"And you were my George McFly," she said.

They both laughed. Then she reached across the table and took his hand and looked him in the eye.

"Seriously, Anton," she said. "You stuck up for me today. Thank you for that. I'll never forget that."

The animal magnetism between them was beyond containment. It was a "check, please" moment you always see in movies.

After dinner, they had a few drinks, and when he dropped her off at her apartment, she invited him in, and the dream date exploded into a passionate frenzy of unquenchable physicality that was beyond anything Anton could have imagined in his most erotic fantasy.

They could not get enough of each other, and when he awoke on Saturday morning under rays of streaming sunlight, Amanda was lying next to him in his arms.

Chapter 7 – Becoming the Mesomorph

He and Amanda ended up spending almost the entire weekend together. It was crazy, Anton thought. Like they were characters in some kind of Hollywood movie.

Things were changing fast, and he was changing fast. His physical form was transforming by the day before his eyes.

Pre formula, his petite five-foot eleven-inch frame was a soaking wet one-hundred seventy pounds. He was what the bodybuilders at the gym would call "skinny fat," meaning small with no muscle and covered by a layer of soft body fat.

On a trip to the grocery store Sunday morning, he stepped up on the giant scale they had out in the lobby, and he weighed in at a rock-solid one-hundred ninety-four.

His body was now a mass of vein-ridden armor. The layer of fat had literally eviscerated. But what he did have all over his body now, especially his formerly baby smooth torso, was hair. Lots of hair.

Anton was worried the hirsutism would turn off Amanda. It had the opposite effect.

"I'm an old school girl," she would say. "All these guys shaved down, It's, well, a politically incorrect term. So, let's just say it's not a turn on. But chest hair? Ummm, yes please."

He could feel the shape of his skull and face changing too. It was not that noticeable yet, but he was certain it was happening.

And there were other changes too. Non-physical ones.

He could think clearer, but he thought differently. He could sense danger—a speeding car about to come around the corner, an approaching storm. He could even sense things about someone just from their smell. Even what kind of person they were, good or bad.

Good or bad. That was how he now saw the humans he encountered. He thought more binary now. There were the people and things he would fight to protect. And then there were his enemies.

When he returned to work on Monday morning, there were two security guards waiting to walk him to his office to get his personal things and escort him off the property.

Roberts and the suits did not waste any time going to bat for their little bitch, Lee Colt. But that was to be expected. Anton had a contract with the University that guaranteed him two years severance. So now that he was with Amanda, it was good riddance to escape from this corporate snake pit. He just wanted to get his things and get out.

But of course, one of the security guards just had to be an asshole about it.

After filling up two boxes of personal stuff, Anton headed for the door, and the full-of-himself-wanna-be cop stepped in front of him.

"Whaohh. Where to do you think you're going, pal?" he said.

"Is there a problem?" Anton asked.

"I need to inspect those boxes," the guard snapped.

"What? You just watched me load them up item by item?" Anton said. "Both of you did."

The guard glared at him.

"Oh? Is that so? Looks like we got us a smart ass here," the guard said to his partner.

"Yeah, a real tough guy," the second guard mocked.

"Put the boxes down," the guard said, smacking up into his personal space. So close, Anton could feel his stomach turn from the fascist's putrid breath and nauseating body odor.

Oh, Anton wanted to push back. My God, he wanted to set this prick straight so bad he was shaking inside. But he just wanted to get the fuck out of here. So, he complied and put down the boxes.

The guard pointlessly rummaged through them, just to be a dick.

"Satisfied?' Anton asked. "So, can I please be dismissed now?"

The guard looked him up and down with sneering disdain.

"Not so fast, pal," the guard said. "I still need to search you."

Both guards broke out into cackling laughter.

Anton had enough.

He locked eyes with the guard and glared at him.

"If you lay one finger on me," Anton said. "I'm going to take this left hand…this one right here…"

He showed the guard his open left palm for emphasis.

"And I'm going knock you clear across the room and into that wall right back over there," Anton said.

Both guards looked at each other and began to laugh again, this time even louder and with more mocking disdain.

"Is that right?" the guard said, still laughing.

"Yeah, that's right," Anton said.

The security guard poked Anton and then smirked.

"Well, it looks like I'm still standing, smart guy."

Anton snapped his left hand forward, driving the heel of his palm into the guard's chest, putting the force of his body behind it with a quick, hard rotation of his core.

The guard flew across the room, smacking into the wall so hard, a cloud of plaster exploded into the air.

The second guard went for his gun. Anton never gave him the chance to get it out of the holster.

He slammed into the second guard sending him across the room and down onto the floor right next to his dazed partner.

Then, Anton gathered up his two boxes and walked out, leaving behind the HUBRC lab forever.

He spent the rest of the morning at Gold's Gym, relishing the feel of the vein-gorging pump before going home to consume everything in sight. Then he face-timed with Amanda, spent some time updating the graphs, charts, and equations that he was using to document his progress on the formula.

After that, he went to the local park.

But today, he did not sprint. Instead, he found himself drawn toward the adjoining wildlife refuge, so he took a walk along the wooden bridge that crossed over the densely forested patch, a peaceful oasis of soothing green amid that suburban sprawl of his South Miami neighborhood.

This was another one of the sudden changes he had documented since being on the formula.

He had never been an outdoor guy before, but now Anton found a soothing comfort in nature and being around and amid the natural world and the creatures that inhabited it. He was now in tune with the cycles and cadences of the Earth. He felt connected to the natural world in a way he never had before. As if he too, like the ancient hominids whose genetic codes were now part of his, were a creature of the forest.

He even had the urge to climb a tree and swing from limb to limb and had no doubt that physically, he'd be able to pull it off now. And be able to locate any edible fruit that might be hanging from its branches.

When Anton had designed the formula, he had made it open-ended. The concept was to create a reverse engineering mechanism that operated at the genetic level, erasing mutations and re-installing old traits that had long faded out of the human genome such as dense bones, physical strength, quick reaction time (and quick thinking), as well as super-sharp senses.

But the formula was broad in scope. It had to be in order to be effective. That meant other changes, side effects such as hirsutism, changes in actual body shape and structures, and probably other effects that Aton admitted to himself he was not quite sure of.

He also had no idea what the end date was. That part of the research hadn't been completed yet when Roberts stole the project away from him. Anton had no idea whether his de-evolution would stop at Homo erectus around one and half million years ago, or continue all the way back the original prototype hominids, or even beyond that.

So as Anton gave in to the joy and fierceness bursting inside him and effortlessly hoisted himself up unto a tree branch, he had no idea where he would end up on the evolutionary timeline. The face and skull growth and reshaping, his hands growing larger and infinitely stronger, the growing body hair and lack of growth of his scalp hair (as Nicholas Wade noted in *Before the Dawn*, "When was the last time a chimpanzee needed a haircut?"), these and other changes were accelerating at an exponential rate.

What Anton had unleashed with his formula was now out into the universe and was taking on a life and path of its own. What did it all mean? Right now, he really did not care. He had spent his entire life overthinking everything. Right now, he just wanted to feel, and he had never felt better.

Not ever. Not even close.

Climbing skyward, swinging from branch to branch, feeling the rush of wind and sun upon his face and body, Anton felt a connection with the world around him, and indeed the universe itself.

His heart soared. He had never felt so alive in his life.

Chapter 8 – The Other Biff

The primal passion fest between him and Amanda went on for several days, with them spending the nights at her place. The more he changed, the better he felt, and his unquenchable desire for Amanda only seemed to bring out her lustful desires as well.

They became intensely connected, physically, mentally, emotionally. But Amanda was not enhanced by a gene therapy formula and needed recovery time.

"I just can't keep up with you," she confessed. "I really need a good night's sleep. I mean going to bed early and actually sleeping."

She laughed about it and smiled, and when he left to head to the door to let her get some rest, he could feel she was going to miss him and that what was happening between them was real. More real than any Amanda fantasy he had daydreamed up during his decades of unrequited love.

But when he returned to his house, waiting for him was the same unrelenting cacophony of noise. The non-stop source of stress that had made his life in that house, such a living hell.

There was a full-blown multi-kegger beer blast raging next door.

Once inside his house, he could literally feel his walls shaking from the pounding bass and the howling screams emanating from Bluto and his frat house of middle-age scumbags.

Anton really did not want to have a confrontation. He did everything he could to take his mind off it and block it out. But it was so insanely freaking loud. It sounded like they were all standing in his living room, screaming in his ear.

He endured the pounding music, and the shrill screams for as long as he could. He really did.

But then, something inside him snapped.

"Enough!" he said aloud to himself as he marched out his front and headed into enemy territory,

Anton arrived at the door to Bluto's screened-in back yard patio, and the first thing that struck him, beside the noise, was just how many screaming, gross, nasty, sweaty, drunken humans Bluto had packed onto the patio. There had to be at least fifty, maybe as many as seventy or eighty people packed onto a space designed for your average size American middle-class family backyard cookout.

They were all so wrapped up in their rage-filled drunken stupor that nobody even noticed him standing there.

He needed a way to get their attention.

He ran back to his house and into the garage to get a regulation size official NCAA football. He kept the football there for the once a year visit he got from his sister and her family, which included a teenage son who played High School quarterback. His nephew was quite good actually and had even coached Anton a bit on proper throwing mechanics.

He dusted off the football, put a few pumps of air into it, and headed back over to the middle-age frat house.

He opened the door to the screened-in patio and eyed up the source of the blaring music on the other side of the pool, an elaborate stereo system of some kind. It was up on a table about fifteen meters away, and he had a clear shot at it.

Anton broke down into a quarterback stance. He hiked the ball to himself and cocked back his left arm into the throwing position.

He eyed up the target stereo again.

Then, he fired the ball with every ounce of rotational core, leg, and arm strength that he possessed.

He unleashed an absolute laser. He could hear the ball whistle, even over the music.

The stereo was instantly destroyed.

It exploded into hundreds of pieces, spraying the drunken fiends with electronic debris and splintered plastic.

There was a uniform scream of shock and confusion.

Anton jumped into the middle of the crowd and stood in a dominant pose with his chest out, and his arms flared out at his sides.

"Enough!" he roared, repeating what he said earlier to himself.

"No more parties!" he bellowed. "Not now! Not ever!"

The dominant alpha pose he struck, the barbaric rage, and that bullet of a throw—the stage had been set, and Anton wanted someone, anyone to step and challenge him. He ached for a fistfight. But would any of these drunken derelicts have the balls to face him? It appeared not.

He scanned the stunned, frozen crowd for his arch-nemesis and finally found him—cowering behind a group of people in the far corner of the patio. The suddenly stone-cold sober partiers scattered like minnows as Anton marched in that direction.

"Bluto!" he said. "Get over here and face me like a man you pathetic pussy coward piece of shit."

Anton jumped and placed his coiled up, ready to fight form directly in front of Bluto. Then he pointed over at the garden hose.

"Trying using that hose on me now. Come on, tough guy," Anton said. "I dare you. I double dare you."

The muscles, the primitive hirsutism, the percolating rage. Bluto must have sensed it.

The bullying loudmouth lowered his head, cowering in submission. Then he pissed himself. Right there on the spot in front of all his worshippers.

Then, Anton watched the man who had been tormenting him for the last two years scamper away in disgraceful humiliation.

But Anton was not done. His uncorked rage had to be released.

He found the biggest slob he could see, a three-hundred fifty-pound asswipe who always took particular relish in blocking his driveway.

Anton grabbed him by his crotch and fat neck, hoisted him up over the head, and threw him into the pool.

"Leave!" Anton screamed.

"Leave and don't ever come back!"

Then, as they scattered, Anton roared. It was the roar of savage rage. It was the roar of an ancient hominid that had not walked the earth for six million years.

It was the roar of something new. Something that Anton was transforming into.

It was the roar of the Mesomorph.

Chapter 9 – A New Place

Anton paced inside his house. He could not get the adrenaline spike from the altercation with Bluto to subside. It was as if the accelerator inside his system was glued to the floor.

He could feel the changes happening inside him at a new, rapid pace. What took days before was now happening almost instantly in real-time.

There was a deep ache inside his jaw and neck. He could feel the shape of his structure changing. He could sense his muscles and bones becoming denser, his ligaments and tendons stronger, his neural connections motor functions faster, his reaction time almost instant.

He wanted to document these new accelerated changes, to do measurements and pictures, to add to his growing data of charts and graphs. But he did not even get the chance to look in the mirror.

Because he was too damn hungry. Downright starving.

Ever since he had gone on the formula, he had been eating like a ravenous adolescent, consuming over ten thousand calories per day. The changes inside him were burning up his glucose, glycogen, and fat stores as fast as he could consume food, and tonight's episode had left him extra depleted. He proceeded to eat everything he could get his hands on out of the fridge.

But as he finished dusting off a box of chocolate protein bars and half a dozen apples while washing it down with half a quart of milk, he felt a sharp tingle all over as his ears picked up an approaching sound moving in on him fast.

Danger was coming.

His newfound instincts were spot on again as the front of his house became engulfed in red flashing lights.

It was the cops. And it looked like they brought three squad cars.

Three cars? Are you fucking kidding me?

Of course. They'll come when that dickhead next door calls after ignoring me for the last two years.

God knows what kind of lie Bluto told them about what happened tonight. Anton needed to get out there and tell his side of the story. The truth about what happened.

He opened the front door, and the two cops standing there jumped back in horror.

The next thing Anton knew, he had a half dozen guns pointed at him.

The cops looked shocked. Taken aback. Confused.

Then, Anton caught his reflection in the window of one of the squad cars, and he could see why.

His transformation had accelerated and gone beyond anything he had anticipated.

Anton was no longer a modern human. No longer of the Homo sapiens species. No longer even of the Homo genus.

He was now—something else.

Chapter 10 – The Next Stage in De-evolution

Anton processed the image of himself reflecting off the car window as fast as he could with six guns in the hands of trigger-happy cops pointed at him.

His physical form had completely morphed. He was the distant, prehistoric past, reborn into present-day suburban America.

He had gone back deep into the genetic history.

Before Homo heidelbergensis, Homo erectus, or any of the Australopithecus species. He was somewhere down the evolutionary path before the Homo/Pan split, where the human and chimpanzee lineage separated. Perhaps he was now the fabled missing link. The unknown creature. The common ancestor of humans and chimps. Perhaps he was back even further than that.

But there was no time to analyze now. He had to explain himself to the cops, and fast, or they would shoot him.

"Officers, it's not what you think," he said. "My neighbor has been…"

His voice was several octaves deeper now. His explanation was falling flat. He was having trouble pronouncing consonants and vowels. It took an enormous effort for him to speak.

It suddenly occurred to him why. It was the same reason apes were taught sign language instead of actual spoken words.

My vocal cords. The shape and position have changed.

It was useless to explain, anyway. Even pre-formula, the cops would have sided with Bluto. They always did.

The cops still looked shocked and confused. But the grips on their guns had eased back, just a tiny bit. This was the only window of escape he might ever get. Otherwise, he would wind up with the same horrific fate of any other non-human ape in this situation. If he wasn't shot on the spot, he'd be caged and shipped off somewhere to be experimented on. He could never let that happen. Not ever.

He leaped up over the cops, used the squad cars as springboards, and launched himself up onto a neighbor's roof before descending down into the darkness of a string of backyards that lined up a canal.

Then he ran.

He ran with speed and desperation, and often, he ran using all four limbs in a knuckle-walking fashion.

He would keep running through the backyards and patches of parks and forests that littered across South Miami. He would run until he reached the Everglades and there he would be safe from the scourge of evil humans,

But he had one stop to make on the way.

He had to try and see her one more time.

Chapter 11 – A Tragic Love Story

Despite all that happened tonight—the altercation with Bluto and his pack of middle-age punks, the accelerating metamorphosis, the cops, the running, his clothes and shoes tearing away from his morphing physical form—despite it all, the Velcro belt and holster he wore to hold his iPhone remained intact, as did the phone itself.

Hiding under the darkness of a giant banyan tree just outside Amanda's apartment building, Anton took out the phone. Though his hands were now twice the size that they were, his manual dexterity remained.

He texted Amanda. Told her to please come down and meet him at the edge of the courtyard. She typed back a string of question marks. Then he typed back, begging her to please come down now, telling her it was urgent.

She was down there in an instant, no doubt worried sick and fearing something horrible had happened.

He texted her again, directing her toward the banyan tree.

She approached. Closer and closer. He could see the panicked look of grave worry on her face.

He called out to her from the darkness of the shadows, praying that she would recognize his voice.

"Amanda," he said. "Over here, by the tree."

"Anton? Is that you?" she said. "You sound different. Are you sick or hurt? What's wrong? Please tell me? Why are you hiding back there?"

She walked into the shadows toward him.

"Please, no, Amanda! Please. I don't want you to see me like this."

But it was too late.

She stood right in front of him.

She stared.

She was shocked at first. Maybe even scared, but then he felt her look into his eyes.

"Anton! Oh my God, it is you," she said.

Then, as she looked at him, Anton could tell she was figuring it out.

"The formula. You already created a prototype, didn't you?" she asked. "And you took it. Experimented on yourself."

"Yes," he said with a straining voice. "I was desperate. This was before you happened. The formula was all I had. I couldn't let them take it from me."

"I expected size, strength, keener senses, a better immune system," he said. "Some hirsutism. But not…not this."

She looked at him, and he could tell she still felt the same way about him. Maybe even more so.

"Then, we'll figure it out," she said. "I'll help you. I'll sneak whatever equipment you need out of the lab and bring it to your house. There has to be a way to reverse the effects."

Anton shook his head in despair.

"It's not possible. The DNA instruction codes are permanent," he said.

"And the police have seen me," he said. "Roberts will find out. Word will go up the chain. Every pharmaceutical fascist and government spy agency on Earth will be looking for me."

"But there has to be a way…" Amanda said.

There was a moment of silence between them.

"Then you came here to say good-bye, didn't you?" Amanda said.

"Yes," he said.

"But where will you go?" she asked.

"It doesn't matter," he said. "But I have to go. It's only a matter of time before they figure out what you mean to me. It's better that you don't know where I'm at."

"Your phone," she said. "You can keep it. I know a way to disable all GPS tracking on it."

"Already done," he said. "It's the first thing I do with every phone I get. Turns out, my being paranoid is paying off."

She looked at him. Looked at him in a way that made his heart ache.

"But Anton…" her words broke off.

"I know," he said. "This last week…being with you. It was the happiest time of my life. If only…"

The sound of approaching sirens sent Anton's danger sense spiking.

"Goodbye, Amanda," he said.

She hugged him and held him tighter than Anton had ever been held before. When she let go, he looked at her, fighting back the urge to howl out and express his emotional pain.

Then he disappeared into the shadows. And he ran.

He ran into the night. Into the woods. Into an uncertain future where he would try to survive as something new. Something from the past.

Dr. Anton Mason was no longer human.

Now, he was the Mesomorph.

www.ingramcontent.com/pod-product-compliance
Lightning Source LLC
Chambersburg PA
CBHW071933120726
48001CB00005B/1954